JUST
DESERTS

JUST DESERTS

JERRY CROWTHER

The Book Guild Ltd

First published in Great Britain in 2023 by
The Book Guild Ltd
Unit E2 Airfield Business Park,
Harrison Road, Market Harborough,
Leicestershire. LE16 7UL
Tel: 0116 2792299
www.bookguild.co.uk
Email: info@bookguild.co.uk
Twitter: @bookguild

Typeset in 11pt Minion Pro

Printed and bound in the UK by TJ Books LTD, Padstow, Cornwall

ISBN 978 1915352 347

British Library Cataloguing in Publication Data.
A catalogue record for this book is available from the British Library.

For Jen

ONE

As they drove into the car park of their local supermarket, Derek Tile experienced a mild sense of disappointment: it wasn't busy; far from it, in fact. Although he hadn't studied the data on weekday traffic volumes in this precise location, Derek suspected it represented something of an outlier event.

'Unusually quiet,' his wife confirmed, 'even for a Monday.' Sandra smiled at her husband. 'At least it won't be crowded inside. Shall we get started?'

'We shall, my love.' He steered the Jaguar saloon to the left and commenced the double circuit generally required on these occasions. Every now and again, following the established protocol of non-verbal communication during an inspection, certain signals were exchanged between them. A tap on the dashboard; a finger pointed; a nod of agreement. Derek would stop the car and Sandra would open the glove compartment. Inside was a stack of yellow cards, laminated and printed with a short message:

When they were satisfied that all miscreant motorists had been identified and issued with windscreen notices, the Tiles selected a bay in the corner with sufficient shade for their terrier Benson (son of the previous dog, Ben). Aware that an example had to be set, Derek was careful to achieve perfect positioning.

In truth, they no longer took photographic evidence or reported recidivists – the parking company had been disappointingly lukewarm when approached, mentioning the financial viability of enforcement and something irrelevant about North Korea. Despite this and several examples of unwarranted verbal abuse, including threats of violent reprisal, the Yellow Card scheme was proving an undoubted success. Offending rates had dropped by a remarkable twelve per cent since its launch three months ago, a statistic that demonstrated their initiative had real value as a force for social good. Twelve per cent greater consideration shown for others by users of the supermarket car park; you could say every little helps.

Inside the building, Mike the security guard had stationed himself at one of the MOPs (Maximum

Observation Positions) by the automatic doors, allowing him to monitor the public entering and leaving the premises, while providing a clear view of the frontline on the retail battlefield: the checkouts.

'Greetings, Michael, any trouble this morning?' Derek enquired when the Tiles stopped for one of their regular friendly chats with the guard.

'Not so far.' He sounded disappointed and continued to scan the store as if watching a slow-motion tennis match. 'Had an urgent directive from management,' he confided, 'about grazing. Our policy is now zero tolerance.'

Derek nodded. 'The practice of customers eating and drinking consumables as they explore the shopping environment, with no intention of paying for them. A form of theft.'

'Grazing is shoplifting, pure and simple,' Mike affirmed. He looked at his watch. 'Time to move. Nice to see you both.'

There was a standard procedure for these trips: Sandra picked and Derek pushed; even that he wasn't entirely trusted with, her hand tending to steer the trolley from the front as if he were incapable of both direction and propulsion. They had experienced a MEM (Marital Emergency Moment) two years previously when Derek attempted to introduce a spreadsheet-based system for supermarket visits; configured around the ten aisles and their fifty most common household purchases, it was an ingenious approach which unfortunately failed to factor in miscellaneous articles such as lemons. The bitter row that erupted during the trial run led Sandra to introduce a separation-based system for sleeping arrangements throughout the next four weeks. Ever since, Derek had accepted his supporting role with equanimity.

The Tiles were making good progress. They had reached the third aisle in less than five minutes, Derek noted, having already ticked off 1A, Vegetables (where Sandra made her usual point of selecting something random, in this case curly kale); 1B, Meat, Fish and Poultry (sausages denied as part of a drive to cut back on items her husband ate too frequently); 2A, Fruit; and 2B, Cheese and Butter (Cheddar denied – see sausages). There was some debate in 3A, Yoghurts, Juice and Milk, over the choice of dessert, the problem arising because they'd booked a few days away so only required one pudding. Raspberry tart or apple crumble? Difficult, each had much to recommend it. Sandra shrugged. 'You decide, I don't mind.'

Derek considered. 'Apple crumble.'

'Oh,' said Sandra, in that surprised/disappointed tone normally reserved for her birthday and 25 December.

'No?'

'I just always find it slightly bland compared to a homemade one.'

'Nothing beats your apple crumble, very true. Raspberry tart it is then.'

'But we haven't had it for a while and I'm not making one before we go.'

Derek found himself stuck in aisle three between a raspberry rock and an apple hard place. He spied something at the top of the cabinet and turned slowly towards his wife, aware it was risky timewise to introduce a third option at this late stage. 'Cheesecake?'

There was a pause. 'Cheesecake,' she agreed.

That's when it happened. They heard her laugh first, although not really a laugh, more of a proclamation. *A horrisonant blare*, thought Derek, as the woman rounded the corner at full tilt shouting into her mobile, like she was speeding down the fast lane with one hand on the horn. 'Go on, it'll be fun! Cornwall? The boys are back from school on the Thursday... yuh... so, we'll go Friday... no, he's flying down a week later...' (Blare of horn.) 'You naughty girl!' She snatched goods from the shelves as she barrelled along, blithely oblivious to the presence of anybody else, and crashed straight into their trolley. 'For God's sake!' she snapped at Derek. 'Are you blind?' With that, she accelerated away, clamping the phone back to her ear. 'Sorry... in the supermarket... yuh, it's an absolute nightmare, full of these bovine creatures getting in the way...' (Blare of horn.) 'They should be!'

The Tiles watched her advance towards 3B, Seasonal, where, this being June, lawnmowers, weedkiller and barbeques were offered for sale. Something appeared to catch the woman's eye, and she stopped to inspect it. Sandra stared, expressionless. 'Rather rude, wouldn't you say, Mr Tile?'

'Extremely. Twice.'

'*Bovine*. That was the word?'

'I believe so.'

'Would it be fair to say that in our field of vision one cow in particular stands out?'

'She certainly does.'

'And what are cows good at?'

'Grazing, Mrs Tile.'

They tracked the focus of their attention down 4A, Pasta, Rice and Sauces, adapting to her frenetic style of shopping, Sandra springing back and forth as if attached to the trolley by elastic; through 4B, Ingredients and Sauces; past 5A and B without a pause; then into 6A, Bread and Cakes, where the opportunity presented itself. She selected an individually wrapped pastry before moving on to 6B, Baking, Eggs and Sugar. Derek touched Sandra's arm. 'In the next aisle.'

'Why?'

'There's a CCTV blind spot by the pet food.'

'How do you know?'

'Michael told me.' A tactical decision was made, and they turned around, retracing their steps so they could enter 7, Household and Pets, from the opposite end, thereby intercepting her at the precise location needed for the manoeuvre.

As they waited by the cleaning products, Sandra noticed her husband staring up at something. 'What's wrong?'

He pointed to the sign overhead. 'Do you know this is the only section in the supermarket not divided into two parts?'

She looked at him. 'I didn't know that actually.'

'Why do you think that is? I mean, why choose to conflate these categories under one heading as opposed to… Cheese, Butter *and* Fruit?'

'I have absolutely no idea, Derek.' She decided to stock up on bleach.

As soon as the target appeared down the bottom, they moved into position, parking their trolley perpendicular to the shelving units with Derek behind so the path was blocked. Sandra made a show of studying the packs of dog food.

She came charging towards them. 'Oh, she hasn't! I've booked the court already! That'll be such a bore if we can't make up a four... would he?' (Blare of horn.) 'Take it in turns with him you mean!'

Sandra stepped into her path. 'Excuse me?'

'What?'

Mrs Tile smiled sweetly. 'Sorry to be a nuisance. Would you mind reading a label for me?'

The woman looked at Derek. She seemed to recognise him. 'Why can't he do it?'

'He's blind.'

'Oh, right.' She spoke into her mobile. 'Hang on, I'll call you back.'

Sandra led her over to the cabinet. 'I can't quite make out the ingredients; the print's too small.'

'Yuh. Fine. Which one is it?' She lifted the box and started reading aloud. 'With tasty chicken and vegetables in gravy composition...' The minute their backs were turned, Derek moved across to the other trolley and picked out the bag containing the single pain au raisin. 'Meat and animal derivatives...' He pulled open the plastic packaging and took a giant bite. 'Vegetables, cereals, vegetable protein extracts...' Chewing as fast as he could, Derek stuffed another large chunk of pastry into his mouth and wrapped up the remaining morsel. 'Minerals, derivatives of vegetable origin...' He crept up behind and slipped the incriminating evidence into her jacket pocket then returned to his starting position.

'Which vegetables?' asked Sandra politely.

'It says a mix of peas and carrots.'

'No sprouts?'

'They aren't listed.'

'Derek doesn't like sprouts. He won't eat them.'

The woman looked at Sandra properly for the first time. 'Derek?' (Blare of horn.) 'That is priceless. You've seriously got a dog called Derek?'

'He's not a dog, he's a person.'

'Yuh, right. Are we finished?'

'Thank you so much.' She went over and took her husband by the hand. 'Derek, there's a box I need you to pick up.'

'Of course, my love,' he answered.

In a potentially disastrous development, it took Mr Tile much longer than expected to locate Mike. He'd circumnavigated the entire store before discovering the guard in the top left corner at the entrance to 10A, Frozen, and approached in a hurry. 'Can I have a quiet word?'

'Step into my office.'

'Witnessed something that might be of interest to you.'

'Suspect shopper?'

'Female customer, late forties or early fifties, eating pain au raisin in aisle seven, then placing the remainder in her pocket, not the trolley.'

Mike took a deep breath. 'We've got a grazer…'

'It looks that way.'

'Would you be able to point this lady out to me do you think?'

'If I'm not mistaken, Michael, at this very moment we'll find her in Wines and Spirits.'

She wasn't hard to spot, loading the trolley with champagne while broadcasting on her phone. 'It's absolutely horrific, she feeds her blind husband dog food…'

The guard nodded. 'Much appreciated. Even with our camera coverage you can't beat a tip-off from an honest member of the public. Of course, it's not an offence until she leaves the premises.'

'And if no payment is proffered for the pastry?'

'Then it's shop theft. That means a nationwide ban from our stores and her photograph circulated to local retailers. Hold on, she's moving.' Mike spoke into his radio. 'Control, this is Zulu Five, over… we've got a code twenty-three in progress… suspect is an IC1 female in white jacket… concealment of item in clothing… Delta, Bravo, Whiskey, Oscar… on my way now.' He turned to Derek. 'They want me outside to make the stop if required.'

As arranged, Sandra was waiting for her husband on a bench in the car park that would provide a ringside seat for the drama about to unfold. 'Grape?' she asked when he sat down.

The guard was standing by the exit on his radio when the woman came through the door. 'I've got eyes on her now.' He moved quickly to get in front of the trolley and cut her off. 'Excuse me, madam, can I just stop you there?'

'Yes?'

'Can you return to the store with me please.'

'What for?'

'I need to speak to you inside.'

'Don't be so ridiculous. What's this about?'

'I believe you have concealed an item that has not been paid for.'

(Blare of horn.) 'Absolute rubbish! I don't have time for this.'

'We need to have a chat somewhere private about an item not on your till receipt.'

9

'What item? Is this some kind of joke?'

'The more you co-operate, the easier this is going to be.'

There was a moment's silence. In the brief interval that followed, the Tiles both had another grape. Aware that other shoppers had started watching, the woman's demeanour appeared to change. She leaned forward and lowered her voice. 'Listen, you stupid little man, my husband's a barrister. Do you really want to lose your job?'

Mike held out his arm. 'This way, madam.'

'You're going to regret this. I'm warning you. If you walk away now, I won't make a complaint.'

'I need you to return to the store.'

'So be it. Where are you taking me?'

'To the holding room. You will be searched and questioned.' He spoke into the radio. 'Control, this is Zulu Five… for your information, I've made the stop. The lady has been captured, over.' They disappeared inside.

In the passenger seat, Mrs Tile sat with her head tilted back, the window open and her eyes shut, sunlight transfiguring her smiling face. The only sound inside the Jag was a contented snore as Benson dozed on his travel rug, the only movement a slight wiggling of Derek's fingers as he adjusted his leather driving gloves. He looked across at his wife. 'You seem happy, my love.'

Sandra nodded slowly. She was imagining the scene in the holding room as the woman emptied out her pockets. 'It's satisfying when people get what's coming to them… sometimes karma needs a little help, that's all.'

'The incident certainly won't do Michael any harm.'

'A good afternoon all round,' she agreed. There was a pause. 'Did we buy tuna?'

On the way out, the Tiles drove past a man loading shopping into a car parked so badly it was almost diagonally across two spaces. Closing the boot, the motorist noticed something on his windscreen; it was yellow, a lucky colour on Mondays in his country. A visitor from rural Thailand, his understanding of written English was limited, although he did recognise the last phrase on the card: "Have a safe journey". Grinning in appreciation, and following village tradition, he placed the protective charm on his neighbour's vehicle.

TWO

Monday evening was known as the NoV (Night of Volunteering) in the Tile household. Sandra assisted at a drop-in centre for the homeless organised by a local charity that provided a hot meal, advice, clothing and the kind of basic human interaction missing from many of their lives. The team took it in turns to cook the meals beforehand, then shared the setting-up, dishing-up, washing-up and cleaning-up at the Quaker meeting house between them. The part she enjoyed most was socialising with the service users throughout the hour and a half the doors were open; the experience ranged from heart-wrenching to hopeful but was always interesting and occasionally jaw-dropping. She would never forget a conversation with a regular visitor called Mark not long after she started. 'Prison changes your view about the law, Sandra,' he told her over a coffee. She'd nodded in liberal understanding. Mark leaned forward for emphasis. 'Big mistake getting rid of Tyburn.'

It was quiet at the drop-in this Monday in June – numbers tended to be lower in good weather – so she spent most of the evening guiding a newcomer through several deliberately impenetrable benefit forms and trying to avoid the leftover chocolate brownies. One of these proved more successful than the other.

Derek helped run a disability swimming club that had an arrangement to use the pool of a nearby leisure centre once a week. The sessions incorporated a broad spectrum of activities from simple hydrotherapy to competitive racing, with an emphasis on all participants enjoying the experience of weightlessly gliding through water at their own speed.

While swimming had numerous benefits for those taking part, involvement with the club had also encouraged Mr Tile to pursue an unexpected goal. At sixty-two, he was proud to be the fourth oldest person in the UK (with or without a beard) to achieve the IQL Level 2 Award in Pool Lifeguarding, Intervention, Supervision and Rescue. As his wife was all too aware, this National Pool Lifeguard Qualification (NPLQ) covered every element of pool rescue technique, lifeguarding theory, first aid and CPR; the course required a minimum of thirty-six hours training and one hundred per cent attendance; assessment included multiple-choice question papers with practical demonstrations of water rescue skills; and on completion awarded a Royal Life Saving Society (RLSS) certificate. Thrillingly, it also entitled the holder to purchase the official uniform of red trunks and yellow T-shirt with "RLSS UK LIFEGUARD" printed across the front and back.

Derek didn't take off his superhero costume for an entire week, even wearing it underneath his suit at work. He spent those evenings patrolling the riverbank, just in case someone got into trouble and he was forced to rip off the anonymous sartorial covering and reveal his extraordinary life-saving powers to an astonished world. Unfortunately, the cold and rain weren't conducive to paddling of any kind; nor would Sandra agree to be rescued. But she did threaten to evict him if the fetid trunks and T-shirt weren't sterilised.

Mrs Tile normally arrived home first and this NoV was no exception. On his return, Derek found her sitting with Benson on the cushion of the bay window seat, staring across the close. 'Everything alright, my love?' he called from the hallway.

'I've invited them round for a drink tomorrow night.'

'That sounds nice.' Mr Tile hung up his coat and was about to head up the stairs when he realised the identity of the recipients was unknown to him. He crossed the living room and peered into the front garden, as if expecting to discover the answer situated somewhere on their neatly strimmed and mown lawn. The bivouac of an indigenous people's council, perhaps.

'He's there again.'

'Is he really?' Derek strained his neck to check the sides of the house.

'You've got no idea what I'm talking about, have you?' Isobars of irritation were traced across her brow as thunderheads darkened her eyes. This was a storm warning, a forecast best not ignored.

'None.'

'Let's start with Sue. Our neighbour. Does that name ring any bells?'

Alarm bells, if anything. She was the psychotherapist who'd overindulged at their Christmas drinks party and asked him if he wanted to talk about his "retention issues". Derek thought that was a bit rich coming from someone who'd been divorced three times. 'I know who she is.'

'Well, Sue's got a new man in her life but something's not right. This Daniel told her he works as an asset manager but doesn't like to discuss it. That's a job in finance, isn't it?'

'Professional investment on behalf of others. It means that in-between visits to Mustique and escort websites he charges exorbitant fees for extremely average returns.'

'You'd expect him to have money then?'

'Undeserved, but yes.'

'So why does Daniel drive that old banger, always wear the same cheap suit and not work in London?'

Derek followed her gaze to the service-shy, scrap-dodging Ford Fiesta sitting on Sue's drive. 'You're right, my love. Something's not right.' He looked at his wife. Knowing the question was redundant, he asked it anyway, simply to watch her reaction. 'Have you got a plan?'

Mrs Tile smiled.

They were in the Jag on the drive, waiting. Benson had been taken for an early walk and was now stretched out on his rug in the back, contemplating the proximity of the picnic he could smell next to him. In the passenger seat Sandra was fully equipped for the mission ahead: binoculars, flask of coffee, notepad, mobile phone turned to camera mode, maps of Reading and the surrounding area in each cardinal direction, grapes. The leather gloves of the driver had already adjusted the rear-view mirror in a smear-free fashion, so it was angled towards the front of their neighbour's house. The time was 07:05, leaving ten minutes for quiet conflagration.

'Why didn't you put my car in the garage?'

Derek was surprised not just by the question but the hostility of the tone. 'I don't know. It didn't occur to me.'

'Didn't. Occur. To. You. No, that would be asking a bit much. In fact, why is your car always kept in there?'

'The insurance. It attracts a lower premium if an expensive vehicle is garaged.'

'Of course. Lucky we can only afford one expensive vehicle in that case. What about when you're not using it, does the insurance stipulate the garage must be free of inexpensive vehicles at those times?'

Feeling increasingly riled by his wife's attack, Mr Tile made a tactical error at this point and slipped into sarcasm. 'I imagine not. But you're probably right, as always, and it would be wise to check.' What he didn't realise was the thistle whose prickles needled him at that moment had its root in a resentment from the previous evening. It had flowered overnight.

When her sister called late on the landline, Derek gave such a perfunctory greeting that Sandra had been forced to assure her (falsely) several times that he wasn't uninterested in talking but simply preoccupied. 'Right. I'm not coming to Wales with you tomorrow unless you apologise.' Silence exploded inside the car like an airbag; it wedged between them.

After several long minutes, Derek semi-capitulated. 'I'm sorry if I've upset you in some way but…'

'Unconditional.'

There was another pause. 'I apologise for behaving in a manner that might be construed as inconsiderate at times, albeit unintentionally.' As Mrs Tile moved her jaw from side to side, deciding if this was palatable, the front door of Sue's house opened. Derek cleared his throat. 'Ladies and gentlemen, this is your chief flight attendant speaking. On behalf of Captain Sandra and the entire crew, welcome aboard Mystery Airlines flight 716AM non-stop service from Culvermead Close to The Unknown. Please make sure your seat backs and tray tables are in their full upright position and that your seat belt is correctly fastened. All portable electronic devices must be set to airplane mode until an announcement is made upon arrival. If you are female, think of our travel trajectory as being like a marriage – initially we will soar towards the sun, then comes the comfortable mid-flight plateau, till finally the inexorable descent into disappointment and resentment. Cabin Crew, doors on automatic please, cross-check and report. Prepare for take-off.'

The captain couldn't resist a quick glance over her shoulder. 'Same suit as before.'

When Daniel had reversed out and driven up the close a safe distance, Derek started the engine and performed the same manoeuvre, following the car as it turned left towards the main road. At the roundabout, the Fiesta took the third exit towards the town centre with the Tiles in pursuit.

After several miles of junctions, more roundabouts, traffic lights and jams, they entered Reading's byzantine, camera-studded one-way system; halfway round this masterpiece of urban entropy, at a point familiar to the driver of the Jag from his daily commute, the considerably less prestigious automobile ahead moved across to the left-hand lane. 'So much for the mystery flight, we appear to be heading for the station,' the marquee motorist muttered.

In fact, the suspect shot straight past it. Sandra said nothing. 'I'm saying nothing.'

They drove for a while through a mouldy area of Victorian family houses long since sliced into clammy flats or repurposed as the sandwiched living spaces known as HMOs. In the middle of this interzone, neither centre nor suburb, on a nondescript road, Daniel turned into a communal drive, parked his car next to several others, then let himself in through the front door of the property. Unbeknown to him, this sequence of events had been captured on camera by his new girlfriend's neighbour from her vantage point across the street.

'That's the first lie then,' she informed her husband. 'The reason he always stays at Sue's, apparently, is because there's building work going on at his house.'

'Ah.' While Sandra studied the map book, jotting down the time and location in her notepad, Derek focused the binoculars on the entrance to the building. 'Eight doorbells, from what I can see. And no builders' vans, or evidence of any work going on. It would appear your concerns were justified. Have we got any chocolate?'

'I think not. What did you tell me yesterday, when I wanted a shortbread finger? "Weight control is elementary; never snack when you're sedentary"... there are some chopped-up carrots for Benson in the bag if you're hungry.'

Fifteen minutes and three carrot sticks later, Daniel emerged from the property wearing boots, heavy-duty black trousers and a faded polo shirt. 'He's changed,' Sandra noted, as the camera clicked on her phone. 'Well, that's the second lie. I don't think too many finance professionals go to work dressed as labourers… there's some kind of logo on his top. Can you see?'

'It's an oak leaf… he's leaving – are we carrying on?'

'Of course… The National Trust. Our friend is full of surprises.' The Tiles tailed their target to the outskirts of town and onto the A329, travelling in a north-westerly direction away from Reading. Sandra looked up from the map she was studying. 'We're on our way to Basildon Park, that's got to be where he works. Do you remember going there years ago with Ben? The flower gardens were beautiful. That Japanese couple took a picture for us by the dahlias.'

'Nice house, let down by disappointing scones and poor service in the café. A no-tip tea room as I recall. The place has a colourful history though – I read about it afterwards. There's a five-year period that particularly stands out… in 1871 the owner of Basildon, Major James Morrison, lost the entire estate at cards to the notorious rake and debauchee Lord Ashcroft. Suffering from syphilitic insanity, this gentleman later married a Hungarian Mangalica sow named Henrietta in a private ceremony one August evening by the park's west lake. According to parliamentary records, Ashcroft was ejected from the House of Lords in 1874 for pleasuring himself in the chamber during a debate on the proliferation of foreign pig breeds in southern England. He died in 1876, leaving everything to his wife.'

'What happened to the house?'

'It became political – Britain faced intense competition from the Austro-Hungarian empire at that time. In one of its earliest rulings, the newly formed Supreme Court annulled the inheritance on the grounds Henrietta was the citizen of a hostile state. The property reverted to the Morrison family, who later founded the successful supermarket chain we know today. You might say that porker saved their bacon.'

On one side of the road was the River Thames, on the other a high brick and flint wall that Sandra recognised as the estate's boundary. 'We're almost there.'

The grade II* listed entrance to the grounds consisted of cast iron gates with spearhead railings, stone gate piers topped by putti supporting overflowing urns of fruit, and flanking walls on either side linked to octagonal lodges decorated with carved panels on each face. Unfortunately, the Tiles had no time to admire this impressive piece of eighteenth-century architecture – Daniel didn't slow down. The only structures Sandra did take in were a black sign with "NT WELOME TO BASILDON PARK" in white lettering and an A-board in front of the locked gates bearing the words "CLOSED. OPENS 10AM".

Half a mile further on, the brake lights of the Fiesta illuminated briefly, and the car jerked sharply to the side, seeming to disappear through the boundary wall. Approaching the location of this magic trick without undue haste, the drivers' driver in the Jag swung his machine over to the right-hand lane then smoothly looped round to the left, steering expertly between two wooden posts that marked the concealed opening of a narrow track in the woods. He pulled over on the grass verge next to a notice with an unequivocal message: "NO ENTRY. STAFF ONLY". Derek was unable to read his wife's facial expression quite as clearly as the sign. 'What next?'

'Well, we can't drive any further and they're not open till ten.' She checked her watch unnecessarily. 'There's a bit of time, so we could go somewhere. Chilfont's not far away. It's a buzzy place full of fun, independent shops and lovely boutiques.'

This description produced a physical reaction in Mr Tile akin to panic:

- racing heartbeat
- feeling dizzy, faint and lightheaded
- sweating, trembling and shaking
- shortness of breath with rapid, shallow breathing
- tingling in fingers and lips with tightness in chest
- rash on upper arms, chest and the complex, combination skin of his face
- nausea

He became fired with sudden enthusiasm for the matter at hand. 'I agree about the car, so we proceed on foot. If nothing else, it means Benson gets another walk.' Involving the dog was slightly low but necessary in the circumstances to avoid the oxymoron of retail therapy.

'And what happens if we get caught?'

'Luckily, my love, we have the broken lead in the boot.'

Even her husband was able to make a connection between the thwarted browsing of independent boutiques and the disdain in her reply. 'The what?'

'We're in the middle of a long journey and need to let the dog out to empty his bladder. He spots something and takes off, snapping the lead in the process. We've only just caught up with him.' This was something of a triumph, Mr Tile believed.

'No one's going to believe that nonsense.'

'I disagree. It's perfectly plausible.' He opened the door and got out.

After ten minutes of traipsing down the track Sandra had had enough. 'Can I have the keys? I'm going back to the car.'

'Okey-dokey.'

'You should be in the woods. If you'd found Benson, you'd be heading in the other direction. If you'd literally just caught him, you'd still be in among the trees. It might be difficult to explain.'

Derek glanced at the tangled undergrowth of thorns, brambles and nettles rising either side of the path; although the reasoning was sound, he (correctly) suspected a vindictive element to his wife's suggestion. 'I'm very sorry, I must've got confused and turned the wrong way. Having a senior moment. Thanks for your help; my wife will be getting worried.'

'I doubt it. She's taken the car and gone clothes shopping in Chilfont.'

'Is that right? Maybe she's forgotten that this entire escapade was in fact her idea and wouldn't actually have been her husband's first choice as a day out had he been democratically consulted about the options avail...'

'What's wrong?'

'Someone's coming.'

Sandra looked round. A vehicle was approaching from the direction of the road. 'OK. We've got Benson and now we're going back to the car. Just keep walking.'

The Land Rover stopped as it came alongside; the letters NT were inscribed on the door. A man of similar age to the

Tiles addressed them through the open window. 'Can I ask what you're doing?'

'Greetings,' Derek beamed. 'We lost our dog I'm afraid. Gave us a bit of a scare. Got him now though.'

'Is that your car parked at the top?'

'It is.'

'So, you saw the sign.'

'We did and had no intention of entering the prohibited area. However, this little rascal spied something in the trees and bolted.' He held up the length of lead where he'd tied it together. 'The useless thing snapped. I guess you get what you pay for.' Mr Tile tutted. 'That'll teach me.'

The man sighed and shook his head. 'Good one.'

'Excuse me?'

'The broken lead story. It's neither true nor original. I hadn't heard it for a while, then we had one on Saturday. And now you. NT doesn't stand for Notably Thick.' He picked up his radio. 'What you're doing is trespassing.'

Mrs Tile made a decision. 'We know Daniel. He said to drop by if we ever came here. Do you work with him?'

The man stared at her for a few seconds then grinned. 'Sandra? It's me, Simon.'

She became visibly flustered. 'Simon... from school?'

'With a bit less hair and a few more kilos than our last meeting.'

'That must have been about forty years ago.'

Simon laughed. 'When you dumped me.'

'No, I didn't! It was mutual. We agreed to split up.'

'You wanted to concentrate on your A levels.' Derek coughed; they both ignored him. 'And in the process broke a young man's heart.'

23

Sandra giggled. 'Rubbish! You went out with Lisa Berry two weeks later.'

'Are you married?'

'I am. You?'

'Divorced.' He grinned again. 'No one was ever good enough after you.'

'Allow me to introduce myself. My name's Derek Tile. I was referenced indirectly just now when my wife, Sandra Tile, mentioned her marital status.'

Simon looked at him. 'OK. Why don't you jump in the back? I'll drop you down at the café. You can grab a coffee and I'll let Dan know you're here. I'm pretty sure the asset management team are working in that area this morning.'

Sandra was all smiles. 'That's very kind. Thank you. What does asset management actually mean? Daniel's never really given me a straight answer.'

'It's a posh way of saying maintenance.' He laughed. 'Don't tell him I said that. To be fair, there's a bit more to it. You've got to know your stuff about listed buildings.'

Behind the Land Rover, Derek tried to stop her. 'What are you doing?'

'Sorting out your mess. Do you want to be charged with trespass?'

'This is not a good idea.'

'Don't worry, nothing can go wrong. We have the broken lead.'

Simon leant out of the car window. 'Why don't you ride up here with me Sandra?'

In the front she settled into the passenger seat and studied the driver. 'I'm getting a sense of déjà vu.'

'You remember my red Mini?'

'I do.'

In the back, Benson looked at Derek. He didn't seem happy.

Ten minutes later, the Tiles were sitting at a table outside in the sunshine, enjoying a coffee with the quiet determination of any normal couple not speaking to each other.

Half an hour later, they were still sitting there. The cups were empty, and the day was heating up, but Derek and Sandra pretended not to notice. Both were furiously absorbed in the displacement activities – a critical appraisal of *National Trust News*, a lengthy reply to her sister's text – which formed an essential strategy in the game of Winning the Silence; as with two evenly matched tennis players, these battles had been known to last for hours.

On this occasion Mrs Tile's frustration finally got the better of her and she put the phone down on the table. 'I don't think he's coming.'

Her husband smiled almost imperceptibly. Victory in the tiebreak. He looked up with a studied nonchalance. 'Sorry?'

'Don't be childish. We can't wait here all day. I'm going to ask in the café.'

Derek returned to an article he'd been reading about Red Squirrel Awareness Week, a subject close to his heart. It highlighted how these creatures were critically endangered by a fatal combination of habitat loss, littering of wild places and ongoing competition from the pox-immune, but infection-carrying, grey squirrel. Reds vs greys; bees vs wasps; dolphins vs sharks. In his opinion, there were many examples of Manichaean division among animals, with one obvious counterpart in the human population: motorists vs farmers. The origins of this antipathy could be traced back to rural Norfolk in the early nineties when a tractor caused a five-mile, two-hour tailback by malevolently refusing to pull over and let the traffic overtake. Eventually turning into the gate of his farm, the bellicose bucolic had parked at the entrance specifically to taunt the queue of seething holidaymakers, including the occupants of a nearly new 1991 Jaguar saloon, grinning and giving them the finger.

This manure-brained boor typified the aggression often encountered by, and perpetrated against, innocent drivers on remote country roads. According to social anthropologists, such openly hostile behaviour had become endemic in certain agricultural communities, arising as it did from the calamitous confluence of undesirable genetic traits, cursory education and a prolonged absence of sexual encounters outside family groups. The only solution seemed to be a radical programme of farm-closing and wood-growing, a policy which, by happy coincidence, would benefit both the touring motorist and threatened red squirrel.

'We've got a problem.' Sandra sat down, looking agitated. 'Daniel's been here. The woman in the café said he came in and ordered a drink. She went to the fridge to get some milk; when she came back, he'd gone.'

Derek was puzzled. 'It's unfortunate but I don't see why it's a cause for concern. Sounds like he got called away.'

She shook her head. 'Too much of a coincidence. I think he looked out of the window and saw us.'

'Maybe, but we've never met. How would he recognise us?'

'It's possible Daniel noticed me yesterday morning. His car pulled out of Sue's drive when I was in the front garden with Benson.'

'Okey-dokey. Let's—'

'Can you not say that? It makes you sound like a talking donkey. A dopey one.'

There were times, two decades later, when Mr Tile still regretted giving up smoking. 'Let's assume the worst. Daniel did recognise you and skedaddled. That means he knows the game's up. Perhaps he'll come clean with Sue, which is a good thing.'

'Nothing's good about any of it!' She held up a spoon. 'There's cutlery on this table with greater insight than you. What it means is, we've lost control.'

Derek regarded the perceptive spoon; it stirred him into action. 'Okey-dokey, Dopey Donkey here. I'm going home to asphalt the small shed. If my role is to be routinely insulted without reason, I have no desire to participate further. The roof of Shed Minor needs some attention.'

Sandra closed her eyes and nodded. The contrite face. 'Sorry if I came across as rude. I'm upset.' She looked away for a moment. 'Sue's a friend of mine. I don't want her to get hurt; she doesn't deserve that. She's a good person.'

'Apology accepted, my love. You were in the wrong and admitted it. An event which future generations will commemorate in the calendar with a public holiday and festivities. Let's move forward, as we always do. Now, I suggest we apply some analytical reasoning to the current situation. Do you have a pen and paper? It seems to me that Dan the Maintenance Man has three choices.' He listed them:

1. Idiotic option – do nothing at all.
2. Honest option – admit his deception without addition or elaboration.
3. Risky option – relate this morning's incident as a way of blurring the issue.

'The third is obviously the least desirable from our point of view. It is also risky for him because, having acknowledged you're a delusional fantasist, how do you convince a psychotherapist her friendly neighbours are following you? We have no way of influencing his decision, as you correctly point out, so how about we collect the car and take Benson for a walk in the grounds?'

It occurred to Sandra there was actually a fourth choice – the nuclear option – which she chose not to think about. 'Sounds lovely.'

After a suitably ambitious expedition around Basildon Park, traversing the woods and fields, taking in two lakes and multiple viewpoints, as well as revisiting the justly renowned flower gardens of the estate, not forgetting to appreciate the maze and arboretum, the Tiles were seated on the lawn in front of the Palladian mansion enjoying their well-earned picnic under (appropriately enough, in a National Trust Experience) an oak tree. Benson had passed out on the rug, too exhausted to place an order for lunch.

Looking up from his second Scotch egg, Derek noticed an animated discussion taking place by the house. It seemed to involve a female visitor and a male member of staff; they were too far away for him to hear the content, but judging by the body language, the tone didn't appear to be amicable. 'Something of a disagreement going on over there,' he mentioned to his wife.

She studied the scene for a moment. 'Maybe he's making a point about all those unsupervised children. She's one of the teachers.'

'Or possibly, she's a member of the public complaining to him about the neglected state of the woodland.'

These had been the two negative aspects of their ramble: random groups of schoolchildren roaming around apparently lost, diffused over wide areas, with no adults in sight (apart from one harassed-looking young man who informed them he was "missing most of Year Five") and, disappointingly, not just the discarded detritus – scattered by anthropoid trash dispensers – the Tiles were accustomed to cleaning up but an entire bagful of tatty, blue and yellow ribbons hanging at regular intervals along tracks in the woods, constituting both an eyesore and a danger to wildlife.

'Do you think that was us subconsciously signalling our new-found commitment to mutual respect and understanding?' Derek asked, offering his wife a grape.

'Do I think what was?'

'The way you took his side and I took hers?'

'What are you talking about?'

'The pair arguing over there.'

She shook her head. 'No. She is a teacher. That was a statement of fact. I heard her on the phone when I took the bags to the bin. I didn't like to contradict you after your overreaction earlier.' She took the grape from his fingers.

Across the lawn, the deputy head and event manager had reached stalemate, repeating themselves with increasing exasperation. 'As I've already stated,' he stated, 'the woodland trails were laid out yesterday. I spoke to the rangers afterwards.'

'Clearly, it wasn't done properly,' she maintained. 'They were incomplete.'

'It was done according to the spec and signed off. A longer trail with blue ribbons for Year Six and a shorter one with yellow ribbons for Year Five. Exactly as the school requested.'

'So why were half of them missing?' She'd never had a school trip go wrong before. 'We've got children wandering all over the place. I just hope nothing happens.'

'I suggest we go down to the rangers' office.' There was no way he was taking responsibility for this fiasco. 'Perhaps they can shed some light on the situation.'

The pair of combatants marched in silence over the grass, past another couple under an oak tree sunlazing in the warmth, a small dog dozing beside them. They didn't notice each other.

It was dark in the bedroom and her phone was ringing. She couldn't locate it properly because Derek was snoring so loudly. The two sounds had synchronised. Answering this call was important. Instinctively, she flung her hand towards the lamp on her left. It struck something hard; there was a groan... Sandra sat up with a start and looked around, gradually getting her bearings. As she picked up her mobile, it pinged: a missed call and text from Sue. *U around? Need a chat*. She considered her response. *In Reading. Will call when back*. Almost straight away, Sue replied. *X*.

Mrs Tile gently shook her husband. 'We need to go.'

He rubbed his chin. 'Did you just hit me?'

'I don't think so. We've both been asleep.' She started packing up.

*

On Wednesday morning, a groundsman would come across the bag of ribbons in one of the bins by the front lawn. Aware of the drama the day before, he informed the event manager, who in turn contacted the school and reported the find directly to the deputy head. At the end of a phone call which started with awkwardness and apologies, moved on to surprise and speculation, then evolved into uncontrolled laughter, he asked her out for a drink. The pair would meet the next week (on the first of many dates) and discover they shared a passion for wild swimming, a taste for pulled pork and an enthusiasm for nineteenth-century European history. At their wedding eighteen months later (dress code: yellow and blue. Food choice: hog roast), the best man proposed a toast to "all the ribbon-snatchers of the world". The happy couple would go on a historical tour of Sweden for their honeymoon, a country with a great flag and nearly one hundred thousand lakes.

THREE

In the car Sandra showed Derek the text exchange, partly to get his opinion, mainly to stop him examining the red swelling on his lower jaw that bore a striking similarity both in size and shape to her engagement ring. 'What do you think?'

'I would suggest it's a reasonable assumption the topic of conversation will be Daniel. And the events of this morning are directly related to Sue contacting you.'

She looked at him in disbelief. 'Is that it?'

'Probably. It seems too much of a coincidence that she'd suddenly need to talk about a different matter entirely.'

'Thanks. Very helpful.'

'Glad to be of assistance, my love. Which means we can rule out option one, Idiotic. And three, Risky, judging by her final message. Not very likely she'd be sending you a kiss if questions needed answering. So, it would appear the maintenance man has chosen to be honest. A highly satisfactory outcome.'

'We don't know that.'

'It's conjecture, I agree but seems—'

'No. We don't know what Daniel does or where he works. Assuming you're right and he hasn't mentioned us.'

'Ah. I see your point.' He stretched his chin towards the vanity mirror again. 'It could be a horsefly bite.'

'Look at me please. Whatever's happened, and it might not be on your list, let me do the talking. Your job is to be supportive. And silent.'

'I get it,' he answered, his eyes focusing on the fourth finger of her left hand.

'You have a tendency to overcomplicate things. At best it's demoralising and at worst a liability.'

Mr Tile didn't believe this was a charge which could be justly levelled against him. If asked about his occupation, for example, he would reply with lapidary clarity that he was a curator of data – SCIA (Senior Consultant Information Analyst) at the DfT (Department for Transport) with AOR (Area of Responsibility) for the DVLA (Driver and Vehicle Licensing Agency) and DVSA (Driver and Vehicle Standards Agency). In his experience, the majority of people felt no need for further explanation or indeed discussion. He was about to object to this second unprovoked assault in less than twenty minutes when his wife announced she needed to meditate and was no longer available for conversation. She put the seat back and closed her eyes.

Derek took advantage of the quiet time on the drive home to think about an ongoing project of his: the concept for a children's book, provisionally titled *Leonard the Lifeguard*. Leonard was a beloved figure in the small coastal community of Culvermead Bay, known for his quiet heroism, general knowledge and modest lifestyle. The door of his shack-cum-workshop was always open, and townsfolk of all ages called in for help and advice, with something that needed mending, or simply to sit on the beach and discuss statistical correlation in optimal transport networks.

The lifeguard rose at dawn every day and swam in the sea throughout the seasons. After breakfast he would check the weather forecast and mark the tide times on his noticeboard, then clear the beach of litter and collect driftwood for a fire in the evening, walking for miles along the sand. He found all kinds of wonderful treasure washed up on the shore, as well as people camping illegally in the dunes. Sometimes they didn't like being fined and moved on.

In the story, Leonard had many amazing adventures involving violent storms, injured dolphins, reckless tourists, terrible shipwrecks, stranded whales, nail-biting rescues, boating disasters and flagrant parking violations, culminating in a dramatic showdown with his arch-enemy, Norfolk the factory farmer, a cruel and greedy individual who mistreated his animals and polluted the bay with run-off from his fields. Norfolk lived in the farmhouse with his sister.

In the final scene Leonard emerged from a raging sea in his iconic red trunks and yellow T-shirt, bloodied but victorious, a lost child held safely in his arms, the crowded beach erupting in cheers. He shunned media interest and refused all offers of reward, choosing to stay and live simply in his shack where he could watch over the place he loved. A small plaque would mark that spot one day.

The block Derek had was Leonard's own domestic arrangements. He'd made the mistake of mentioning the plot's outline to Sandra, who opined that there was something inherently suspicious about an unsupervised crank living by himself in a shed; concerned residents would be more likely to regard this loner as a potential pervert than a trusted guardian of public safety. Her solution to this problem was the introduction of a new character, Susan the nurse, Leonard's friend. While not a bad idea per se, it quickly became apparent the book's centre of gravity would be irrevocably shifted with this narrative addition; were it not for the smart, capable Susan, the person who really got things done, Leonard would be exposed in public as the bumbling irritant she knew him to be in private – was it any surprise he doted on her, while she sensibly chose to keep her distance? In fact, Sandra proposed the title should become *Leonard the Lovesick Lifeguard*, in which whole chapters were devoted to his grovelling pursuit of the unobtainable Susan. There appeared to be no obvious compromise available that would retain the benefits of this character without changing the story.

Just as he prepared to turn off the A329 and onto the A155, taking a slightly longer route distance-wise but avoiding Reading town centre, inspiration struck Mr Tile: Susan was dead; she had drowned in a freak accident years before and that was why Leonard became a lifeguard. It explained his circumstances and the tremendous affection he was held in by the people of Culvermead Bay; everyone knew, but he never spoke about this tragedy, and no one ever asked him. Derek felt rather pleased with himself.

In the passenger seat, Mrs Tile opened her eyes and regarded her husband with suspicion. 'What are you grinning about?'

'Just in a good mood, my love, it happens occasionally. The GP said it's nothing to worry about. Perfectly normal, apparently.'

She was unconvinced. 'Not with you it isn't. Can you take the next right? I need to call in at work. It won't take long.'

He did as he was asked and turned down towards the Royal Berkshire Hospital, reluctantly accepting the unplanned diversion without (audible) comment.

In the staff car park, Derek watched her disappear through the side entrance of the East Wing on her way to the Administration Department. Bitter experience had taught him that you needed to multiply the PWT (Predicted Waiting Time) by about four to calculate the AWT (Actual Waiting Time); thus, when his wife had stated "I'll only be five minutes" as she got out of the Jag, he extrapolated this to mean nearer twenty.

Unwilling to sit in the car for the duration, Derek decided that some of this hiatus could be constructively filled by taking Benson on an inspection round the outside of the building. He'd completed three quarters of an uneventful lap, noting some minor structural issues to mention in an email to the (always grateful) management team, when he turned a corner to find a young couple outside one of the emergency exits. The man was in a wheelchair wearing a hospital gown with a cast on his leg; she was clearly visiting – both of them were in the process of lighting cigarettes. Mr Tile didn't break stride as he approached. 'Greetings, how are we both?'

They glanced at each other. 'Alright,' she answered.

'How's it going?' the patient asked.

Derek looked round theatrically. 'This is the smoking area, is it?'

The man shrugged. 'Don't know. We are anyway.'

'Yes, I can see that,' Derek responded. 'I think you'll find that smoking is not permitted anywhere within the hospital grounds. Ample signage has been provided so I suspect you are fully cognisant of that fact.'

There was a momentary pause in the conversation during which the other participants stared at him. 'Who are you?' the woman asked.

'I am a responsible citizen who understands there are circumstances when public health outweighs personal freedom. No doubt you are familiar with the ethical debate. Unfortunately, enforcement becomes necessary when individuals, such as yourselves, choose to flout the resulting regulations.'

The man grinned and spoke to his girlfriend. 'That's cheered me up. I thought I had problems.'

'You having a laugh?' she asked Derek.

'Not at all. Now, I'm asking you politely to extinguish your cigarettes or take them outside the main gate.'

The woman pointed at the cast. 'What do you think that is? Steven's only got a broken leg.'

'Seriously, mate,' Steven interjected, 'you're really good. You should go on tour.'

'How's he supposed to get all the way out there?' she demanded.

'The same way he got all the way here, I imagine. In the wheelchair with you pushing it.'

This didn't go down well. 'No chance. I'm not going anywhere. You're the one pushing it, Grandad.'

Derek considered the suggestion. 'Alright, if that's what you want.' He handed her the lead. 'You can bring Benson then.'

Steven found this hilarious. 'Benson? You got a cat called Hedges as well? Bet you're an ex-smoker, they're always the worst. Why don't you do us all a favour and just have one, mate?'

'Come along, Steven, we're going for a little ride.' Derek seized hold of the wheelchair and started propelling it down the path at considerable speed. 'Keep up at the back there.'

'Get off, you nutter!'

'No more illicit smoking for you.' As they reached the end of the block, Mr Tile unexpectedly performed an abrupt U-turn, racing back in the opposite direction. He'd spotted his wife walking across the car park. 'There we go, seems to be running smoothly now. Enjoy your afternoon.' He took Benson and effected his own emergency exit.

The woman took a last drag on her cigarette. 'That bloke needs a tag on him.'

'Come to the wrong kind of hospital I reckon.'

Sandra was waiting for him by the Jag. 'What were you doing over there?'

'Extending citizens advice. Nice couple. Shall we go home now?'

The Tiles were sitting at the kitchen island, affectionately known as Madeira (as in, "every morning we have breakfast on Madeira Island"), enjoying a well-earned cup of tea after their eventful day out. Sandra had carefully considered her strategy. 'I'm going to give Sue a call in a minute. I think it's best if we talk at hers.'

'Good idea. After Eights or Kit Kat?'

'You've lost me.'

'Sue likes chocolate. I thought it might be a nice touch if we took some round with us. Those are the two choices currently available.'

She shook her head vehemently. 'Absolutely not.'

'As you wish, my love. Digestives?'

'No. You're not coming. That's the last thing I need. There must be a job that needs doing. Didn't you want to work on the shed roof?'

Derek looked at his watch. 'Bit late to start a project like that. It's gone four.'

'Can't help I'm afraid. You're just going to have to entertain yourself for a couple of hours.'

He made a quick calculation as she left the room. 'Around midnight.'

Deciding to check the route for the final part of their journey the next day, Mr Tile went to collect the map book from the car. He opened the front door to find their neighbour coming up the drive; she was wearing dark glasses and holding a bottle of wine. As she approached the house with a definite intensity of purpose, not waving or smiling in recognition, he could hear her phone ringing. 'Greetings, Sue, how are you?'

'Hello, Derek. Not having a great day actually.'

'Sorry to hear that… aren't you going to answer it?'

'No. I don't want to talk to anyone.'

'I think you'll find it could well be Sandra.'

'Well, I'm at your house now.'

He twitched. 'Sandra doesn't know you're here though, does she?'

'She will in a minute.'

An involuntary spasm shook his body. 'The point is, at this precise moment, nobody other than myself is aware of your presence on our doorstep.'

'I'm not in the mood if you're having some kind of OCD attack.'

'I'm going to have to ask you to hand over the phone if you don't mind, Sue. I've tried to be reasonable, but if you don't want to take the call then I'll have to answer it myself.'

The ringing stopped. 'Can I come in now?'

'Of course, feel free to enter... I see you've brought some wine. That's very kind. Bit early for me normally but I suppose we are technically on holiday.' He called up the stairs. 'Guess who's here? It's our neighbour Sue! She's come round with a nice bottle of white wine!'

Sandra appeared on the landing. 'I've been trying to...' She took one look at Sue and immediately turned to her husband. 'Why don't you put that bottle in the fridge and then go and mow the lawn?'

As he sat in Shed Major considering the various jobs on his list, none of which it made sense to start at 16:30 the day before going away, Mr Tile wondered if his wife was getting forgetful. He'd spent the entire previous morning engaged in sward management – a more accurate term, in his opinion, to describe the sequence of events involved than the single action implied by *cutting the grass* or *mowing the lawn* – and at the time she seemed to be fully aware of the fact, dispensing refreshments and encouragement as he worked. In fact, Sandra had carried out a lengthy inspection of both the front and back gardens when he'd finished, suggesting a surprisingly limited number of amendments and expressing a remarkably large amount of appreciation. All of which proved beyond doubt that cognitive registration had taken place. And yet, here she was, less than thirty hours later, proposing he repeat the exact same process again.

Like many bearded men of a certain age who find themselves alone in a wooden hut with something on their minds, Derek had reason to be grateful for the internet. He typed in *how do I know if my wife is losing her memory?* and was directed to an NHS website about dementia. There was a checklist of seven indicators to look for:

1. *Struggling to remember recent events but easily recalling things that happened in the past.*

This was worrying. Taking just that day as an example, Sandra appeared to have forgotten what happened in her own garden the previous morning but not the Japanese couple taking their picture in Basildon Park's flower garden years ago. Remembering things in the past was definitely not a problem for her, particularly – and this could be down to sheer volume – those which reflected badly on him. In truth, the recall function of her memory computer was the envy of autocratic regimes the world over, with its unrivalled ability to access incriminating files of evidence from long-term storage at a moment's notice.

2. *Struggling to follow conversations or programmes on TV.*

"You've lost me". These words were uttered by his wife less than an hour ago during a routine discussion about calling round on their neighbour. At the time he had considered this to be a misunderstanding about comestibles, but with hindsight a more sinister interpretation of the statement revealed itself. A version in which Sandra had been struggling to follow the actual conversation. Against this, Derek had to admit he was slightly confused about aspects of that episode, not least his own exclusion from the proposed visit to Sue's.

The second part was hard to judge as they didn't spend much time in front of the television together. He thought of two main reasons for this:

A. Sandra refused to have him in the same room during one of her programmes – watching with audio description would be less irritating, apparently.
B. Sandra (inexplicably) never wanted to see another documentary about the Second World War (Battle of Crete/North African campaign/Normandy Landings in particular), the development of Britain's transport network (Bristol Airport/M25/East Coast rail line in particular) or the tireless work of the Red Squirrel Survival Trust (Combating the Grey Menace in particular).

3. *Repeating things or losing the thread of what's being said.*

An occupational hazard in the profession of marriage, as far as Derek was concerned. More a sign of normality in a long-term relationship than cognitive corrosion, although after a certain number of years, perhaps these amounted to the same thing. He began to suspect that his wife wasn't presenting with early onset dementia at all, a diagnosis confirmed by the remaining symptoms listed:

4. *Forgetting the names of friends or everyday objects.*
5. *Having problems thinking or reasoning.*
6. *Feeling anxious, depressed or angry about memory loss.*
7. *Feeling confused even when in a familiar environment.*

It crossed his mind that most of the warning signs mentioned in the article would describe the average denizen of Reading town centre on a Saturday night. Wary of attempting to make the data fit a theory, a cardinal sin in his working life, Mr Tile returned to the empirical evidence. His wife had asked him to perform a task that she'd witnessed him complete the day before; sticking to the facts, he searched online for short-term memory loss.

Transient global amnesia (TGA) was not something he'd come across before. It sounded suspiciously like a phenomenon in some terrifying sci-fi movie about the dystopian future awaiting mankind (called, for example, *Rise of the Planet of the Farmers*) but was in fact the medical term for a sudden, temporary episode of memory loss. It usually occurred in people aged fifty to seventy, had no known cause or lasting effects and required no specific treatment. Characterised by an inability to recall the recent past or store new memories for a limited time, the condition gradually cleared of its own accord with complete recovery in most cases; it only rarely recurred. While the neurological origins of TGA remained disputed, doctors had identified various events as potential triggers for an attack. Derek ruled out some – head injury, invasive medical procedures, sexual intercourse – that, as far as he knew, his wife hadn't experienced in the last few days and others – physical fatigue, emotional or psychological stress – that he knew she experienced most days. The one possible explanation which made sense was sudden immersion in cold or hot water: Sandra had developed an itchy skin rash on her arms and legs after spending Sunday afternoon peeling ivy off the back of the house in the sunshine; having tried various creams and lotions to no avail, she plunged into a freezing bath out of sheer frustration. It seemed plausible to him that the shock of the water affected the brain – specifically, the hippocampus, which wasn't Latin for an overweight holidaymaker pitching a tent, he discovered – in some unexplained way and precipitated the episode of amnesia which followed.

Although hospitalisation wasn't necessary unless the condition continued, common after-effects of TGA to watch out for included confusion about the time during, following and sometimes preceding an attack. There had been reports of sufferers attempting to construct false memories to explain this period, a coping mechanism often expressed with convincing conviction and a natural result of the psychological need for coherence. It was important to recognise that this reflex arose from fear and embarrassment; a profoundly disorientating experience, the emotional effects needed to be handled with sensitivity and understanding. Derek wondered if there were support groups with regular meetings – Amnesiacs Anonymous –

or if they'd tried this and no one remembered to attend.

The majority of people slowly began to recall events and circumstances during recovery, a process which should be encouraged but never rushed. Quite simply, the greatest assistance a loved one or friend could give in this situation was to provide a clear, linear narrative of what actually happened in as much detail as possible. This might require patience, he noted, as not everyone welcomed intervention or help; indeed, cases had been recorded where the existence of a problem was refuted, attempts to correct a false reality rebuffed and the resulting chances of a full return to normality reduced. Denial tended to move through three distinct phases:

1. Amusement and ridicule
2. Dismissal and rejection
3. Anger and accusation

Faced with resistance of this kind, it was important to remain calm and consistent, to pursue the removal of imagined events before they became fully fledged beliefs and to discourage anything that might inhibit the ability to form and store new memories. Like white wine.

Unfortunately, her husband was wrong about Daniel. It transpired he'd chosen the nuclear option which Sandra had feared, unceremoniously dumping Sue by text. *Not working between us. Best we don't see each other again. Don't call. Sorry.* That was it; he'd sent the message and turned his phone off. A messy post-mortem had been conducted on the Tiles' brand new (Benson-free) sofa over the course of the last hour, placing the hostess in an extremely uncomfortable position. She'd managed to negotiate a potential minefield of fatal missteps and explosive revelations, dispensing consolation and condemnation with the same care as the dry-roasted peanuts now being measured out into two small bowls.

She was about to leave the kitchen when Derek came in through the stable door from the garden; walking straight over, he squeezed her left arm as if examining the muscle tone of a horse. 'Do you feel weakness or numbness on either side of your body?'

'I didn't a minute ago.'

'Are you having problems with balance or coordination?'

She laughed. 'Ask me again after the next bottle... is everything alright?'

He looked at her intently. 'Do you remember that bath you had?'

'When?' She raised her eyebrows. 'Have you been thinking about me in the bath?'

'The cold one on Sunday night.'

'I don't know what you've been doing out there, but can you not act so strangely please? My head's spinning already.' She lowered her voice. 'Daniel's ended it with Sue. No explanation... she seems to be coping at the moment.'

Mrs Tile picked up the bowls and walked back into the living room. Derek heard Sue ask her a question, then his name being mentioned and both of them laughing.

Amusement and ridicule: the first phase of denial.

Making a decision to start the programme of treatment without further delay, he opened the fridge; there was about a third of the bottle of white wine left. He poured himself a large glass and took the remainder through with him. 'Here we are Sue, ready for a top-up? Might as well finish it.'

'Don't I get any?' Sandra asked, tilting her glass.

'Not going to help if you're feeling dizzy, my love.'

'Feeling what?'

Sue was concerned. 'That doesn't sound good. I didn't know you got dizzy spells, Sandra.'

'Just a slight problem with her head spinning,' Derek explained. 'She finds it best to avoid alcohol when it starts. Tea with sugar normally works.'

'There's nothing wrong with me,' Sandra stated categorically. 'No numbness, lack of coordination or dizziness.'

'Glad you're feeling better, my love. But drinking some sugary tea would be advisable. There's no need to feel embarrassed… let's ask Sue, if you'd like a second opinion. Have you got a moment, Sue?'

'I'm still sitting here. I haven't been somewhere else for the last twenty seconds.'

'We were just wondering what you'd recommend for Sandra, in the circumstances?'

'A bath, Doctor Derek. Have you thought about that?'

Sandra stood up, laughing. 'I'm going to Madeira, plenty of wine there.'

It dawned on Mr Tile that he needed to enlist Sue's help if the necessary conditions for forming and storing new memories were going to be met; this would require an explanation about TGA and the recovery programme. When Sandra had left the room, he turned to their guest. 'I wanted to talk to you in confidence for a moment, as a therapist.'

'I'm sure that can wait… I doubt it would help anyway. There's not much the profession can do for you at this stage.'

He looked towards the kitchen. 'It's a matter of some urgency.'

'Not everything's about you, Derek; other people have problems as well. I've got a question to ask first, something that's bothering me. I'd like an answer from a male perspective. You need to think back to the dark ages before you were married. Have you ever ended a relationship that you didn't want to?'

There had been one occasion, sleep-depriving at the time. Early in his career, Derek worked for a family run engineering business where he'd been tasked with procuring an important piece of new machinery. Over many years the company's directors had favoured one manufacturer, establishing close personal connections between the two firms. At the end of the tendering process, it became clear a number of other submissions were more competitive; reluctantly, he'd recommended that a different supplier be awarded the contract. He wasn't quite sure why Sue wanted to know about this. 'Once. It was a very difficult situation.'

'What made you do it?'

'There were several better offers.'

'Several?' Sue tried not to sound incredulous.

'That's how it works. You specify your requirements with clear and objective evaluation criteria then proceed with the lowest-cost provider.'

'I see. Charmingly put, Derek. Romantic almost. No emotional considerations then?'

'Not from my perspective. But the relationship involved

the father and both daughters. It had worked well for a long time so there was pressure on me to continue with it.'

'Right.' Sue nodded slowly. 'Glad I asked. What was it you wanted to talk about?'

'Let's imagine someone, not a million miles away at this moment, developed a coping strategy to deal with an intractable problem, then—'

'Could anyone blame her? I think you'd have to, in the circumstances. Must be a nightmare for her.'

He was astonished by this. 'You've noticed as well?'

'Noticed what?'

'The short-term memory loss.'

Mrs Tile reappeared with a bottle and filled Sue's glass. 'This is our wine.'

'Thanks. So, you've been out and about today...' She glanced at Derek. 'Go anywhere interesting, Sandra?'

'Not really, just pottering round Reading. Called in at work on the way home.'

'Anything else you remember about the day, my love?'

She gave her husband a quizzical look. 'You had an encounter with that couple outside the hospital. He was in a wheelchair.'

'We visited somewhere prior to that.' He jumped up and left the room, returning moments later brandishing his copy of *National Trust News*. 'The historic estate of... Basildon Park! We had a long walk and a picnic in front of the house.'

'That sounds lovely; I haven't been there for ages,' Sue commented.

Sandra smiled thinly. 'Yes, it was nice. I'm hoping we'll have some sunshine in Wales this week too. The forecast looks quite good, might even get a dip in the sea if we're lucky.'

'Not a planned visit though, was it?' Derek continued. 'We had no idea where we were going to end up.'

She shook her head, maintaining eye contact with him. 'No. You need to be careful. One wrong turn can lead anywhere. You don't know where it might be taking you. We went to Basildon Park on a whim.'

'I wouldn't call it a whim, my love. On a mission, more like. All your idea, in fact. Is it coming back to you now?'

'Stop being so ridiculous. I don't know what you're talking about. Have you been sniffing Cuprinol again? Sue doesn't want to hear every detail about our day from the moment we got up. I can't imagine why you think it's interesting to anyone else. Please change the subject.'

Phase two: dismissal and rejection.

Patience was required, Mr Tile reminded himself; the greatest assistance he could provide was a clear, linear narrative of the actual events. 'I know this isn't easy for you,' he informed his wife, 'but we're going to work through those details you're afraid of together. Fortunately, Sue's here to offer support as a friend and, if necessary, in a professional capacity. Let's start at seven hundred hours, any recollection of our location at that time?'

Sandra's eyes narrowed. 'I imagine I was in the kitchen. Drinking a glass of hot water with lemon, as I do first thing every morning.'

He shook his head. 'We were sitting in the car, waiting for Daniel to leave.'

'What absolute rubbish! You were still in bed,' she insisted. 'You hadn't made it into the shower, let alone the car.'

'Hang on a minute,' Sue interjected, 'why would you be waiting for Daniel to leave?'

'Exactly.' Sandra swigged her wine on the new sofa. 'Why on earth would we be doing that, Derek? I don't know what happened when you were outside, but ever since you've been experiencing some kind of alternative reality.'

He remained calm and consistent. 'You wanted to find out where Daniel worked. You were suspicious about him. Do you remember that? We waited for his car to pull out of Sue's drive and then followed him.'

Sue sprayed her wine over the new sofa. '*You did what?!*'

'Daniel went to his flat first, where he changed out of his suit. After that we tailed him along the A329 out of Reading to Basildon Park. They know him there as Dan the Maintenance Man.' He picked a phone up from the occasional table. 'You've got lots of pictures, my love. It might jog your memory to go through them.' He held the screen up to show his wife. 'Daniel in his work clothes, outside the building where he lives. That was taken by you. Ring any bells at all? We were sitting in our car across the street. He was under surveillance...'

They were in the garden: Benson because the neighbours' Birman cat had been lounging provocatively on the lawn, in full view of the French windows, as if taking in a summer recital at the Paris Conservatoire; Derek because he'd been locked out.

Anger and accusation proved to be an accurate description of phase three, Mr Tile reflected in the rattan chair. A verbal firestorm had swept through the living room, leaving those engulfed hoarse and red-faced from the blaze.

Sandra's memory had come back; judging by what he'd heard, it seemed unlikely Sue would anytime soon.

The key turned in the latch; the doors opened; and his wife walked out on the terrace. He felt her hands resting on his shoulders as she stood behind him and spoke. 'Let's not talk about what happened. Tomorrow's the start of our holiday... we tried our best, but it's been a lesson I'm afraid.' She paused for a moment and Derek waited for the closing cadence. 'Sadly, some people won't forgive you for helping them.'

*

In August the following year, on a camping holiday in Cornwall with his girlfriend, a ranger at Basildon Park, Daniel would go metal-detecting in the afternoons. On the third day the genial farmer suggested he try a particular field where his uncle had once ploughed up some interesting pieces. An hour later, Daniel uncovered what would come to be known as the "Mawes Hoard", one of largest finds of Anglo-Saxon coins in a century. The collection was acquired by the British Museum with both detectorist and landowner receiving nearly three million pounds. Daniel would invest part of the money in the stock market and successfully manage his own assets for many years.

FOUR

As founder and coordinator of Close Watch, the neighbourhood watch vehicle for Culvermead Close with its all-powerful steering committee, Mr Tile had one civic duty to perform before he could depart for Wales. The WGM (Weekly General Meeting), which normally took place on Wednesday evening, had been moved to the morning. This significant rearrangement of the schedule was achieved with a minimum of fuss and bureaucratic delay – a single phone call to the Milks (both retired) had been sufficient to convene the entire committee (Derek, Geoff and Hilary Milk) for the EWM (Extraordinary Weekly Meeting) at a change of venue (The Milks', Sandra was packing) – underlining, according to both the deputy coordinator (Geoff) and permanent secretary (Hilary), just what a mobile, flexible organisation Close Watch continued to be. It was little wonder they enjoyed such unparalleled success in *driving away crime* (mission statement).

Derek cleared his throat. 'Coordinator concludes. Committee is satisfied that all items in Section One: Recorded Incidents have been dealt with in chronological order, subject to due process. There were no items. It is now proposed we move on to Section Two: Community Events. Coordinator enquires. Is anything coming up in the next week that we need to discuss at this meeting?'

'Secretary responds. One event anticipated.'

There was a short pause. 'Well, what is it?' Geoff asked.

'You're supposed to say, "Deputy enquires" before the question,' Hilary answered.

'Coordinator responds. Secretary is correct on the point of procedure. I would like to remind committee the purpose of the protocol is to assist with the taking of minutes. Since Hilary is our stenographer, we must make her job as easy as we can.'

'Deputy responds. Apologises to Secretary. Deputy enquires. What is the anticipated event?'

'Secretary responds. Visit of Thames Water on Friday to carry out routine maintenance. Partial closure of road for three to four hours.'

'Coordinator enquires. Have Thames Water been made aware all operatives must carry clear identification and that smoking, swearing and the reading of tabloid newspapers are prohibited activities within the communal areas of the close?'

'Secretary responds. Confirmation of email received.'

'Coordinator concludes. Committee is satisfied that all items in Section Two: Community Events have been dealt with in chronological order, subject to due process. There was one item. It is now proposed we move on to Section

Three: Property and Residents. Coordinator enquires. Any planning applications, new arrivals or impending departures?'

'Secretary responds. Potential new arrival at number three.'

'Deputy enquires. At Sue's, really?'

'Secretary responds. His name's Daniel. It's been going on for a while, apparently. I'm so pleased for Sue. She seems very happy.'

'Coordinator responds. I think you'll find that particular relationship is now over. With the caveat I'm not the original source of the information relayed to committee.'

'Deputy responds. It can't be over already – they only got together a minute ago! Any idea what... sorry, I've done it again. Deputy apologises to committee. Deputy enquires. Do you know what happened?'

'Coordinator responds. I was told Daniel ended it.'

'Secretary responds. Oh dear. She's scared another one off.'

'Deputy responds. I would like to express my sadness that nice Sue has gone from being single-no-more to single-once-more in such a short period. Deputy enquires. Should we send her a card?'

'Secretary responds. And say what exactly, Geoffrey – everyone in Culvermead Close is sorry to hear you're single again?'

'Deputy responds. Previous reply was a question and therefore incorrectly phrased.'

'Coordinator concludes. Committee is satisfied that all items in Section Three: Property and Residents have been dealt with in chronological order, subject to due process.

There was an item, but it didn't last long. It is now proposed we move on to Section Four: Miscellaneous Security Issues. Coordinator enquires. Do we have any subjects that need to be raised for discussion?'

'Deputy enquires. Does Coordinator still have concerns about the occupant of number four?'

'Coordinator responds. The records of this committee clearly demonstrate that the opinions and behaviour of Mr Gary Henman represent an ongoing security risk.'

'Secretary responds. What I find upsetting is the way he has tainted the People's Champion by association. Unforgiveable to take the name of Henman in vain.'

'Deputy enquires. Isn't he a lecturer of some kind?'

'Coordinator responds. He is. Gary Henman – Gaz, as he likes to be known – works at the university. A tutor in the philosophy department.'

'Secretary responds. Really useful.'

'Deputy responds. Brain in a van, that sort of thing.'

'Coordinator responds. The rejection of car ownership in favour of a pushbike raises the most obvious red flag about Mr Henman's sanity and intentions.'

'Secretary responds. He carries off the Lycra quite well though, it has to be said.'

'Deputy enquires. Does Coordinator agree that an immediate Community Monitoring Order would be an appropriate course of action?'

'Coordinator responds. He does. There can be little doubt that our friend the pedalling pedagogue is fully deserving of a CMO, in the circumstances.

'Secretary responds. Secretary agrees and doesn't mind watching him, if instructed by committee.'

'Coordinator responds. Original motion carried. CMO for the cycling sophist. Coordinator concludes. Committee is satisfied that all items in Section Four: Miscellaneous Security Issues have been dealt with in chronological order, subject to due process. There was one item. It is now proposed we move on to Section Five: Neighbourhood Matters. Coordinator enquires. Any points of interest to consider?'

'Deputy responds. I've got an interesting question for committee.'

'Secretary responds. I've got some courgettes for you, Derek, don't let me forget.'

'Deputy enquires. Does the Disaster Action Plan allow for the detention of individuals in certain circumstances?'

'Coordinator responds. In the event of an emergency the DAP authorises the Close Watch steering committee, under the terms of our constitution, to apprehend residents regarded as a security threat. This would involve incarceration in a temporary holding facility for as long as deemed necessary. To ensure legitimacy, any such action taken must fall within the scope of the powers granted to us and be subject to the oversight and democratic scrutiny of committee at all times.'

'Secretary enquires. What makes a good holding facility, in case something happens while you're away?'

'Coordinator responds. Ideally, a room in the house that can be locked from the outside.'

'Deputy responds. Like our porch, Hilary. During an emergency, both doors could be secured. It would be quite straightforward. With the inside already locked, we'd show any bolshie resident into the porch – "After you Gaz" – then simply turn the key on the outer door behind him. Job done.'

'Secretary responds. That's not very fair, Geoffrey. I couldn't live with that. We'd have to go through the back all the time if we had a philosophy tutor detained in the porch. The utility room would suit Gary Henman better. He'd be much more at home in there, watching the machines go round, plenty of cycles to think about...'

Half an hour later, Mr Tile left the meeting and walked the short distance across the close to his house. He carried with him the burden of responsibility for his neighbours' security and a bag of courgettes. His wife was waiting in the living room with a card in her hand. 'Hope it went well. Could you sign this?'

Alerted to a potential ambush by the absence of any time-based reprimand, Derek read the message inside. It was to Yvette, Sandra's sister; apparently, she had a birthday. 'Why does it say "see you on Friday"?'

'Because we're going to be in the Gower. They live about an hour from where we're staying. It would be nice to visit them for lunch. Please don't start being difficult; we've got a long journey.'

There were many adjectives which would render the penultimate sentence more accurate – it would be rebarbative to visit them for lunch, to take one example – but the implicit threat of a three-hour road trip in complete silence persuaded him to add his signature to the contract without further comment. 'Did you put my suit in for Monday?'

'Yes, and your work laptop.' She picked up the bag. 'More of Hilary's courgettes. Perhaps you could give them to Yvette – she makes chutney.'

Derek thought of the arrayed pots of pungent compost they received at Christmas every year, gumming up the larder like a row of rotten molars. 'Not for human consumption, she doesn't.' Sandra didn't say anything but gave him a look – tolerant, sympathetic even – that spoke quite clearly of mission accomplished: grumble all you like, you're signed up for Friday; I have your consent in writing.

Apart from a brief diversion to post Yvette's card at a box Sandra knew had a midday collection, the Tiles drove non-stop for one hour and forty-eight minutes from Junction Eleven on the M4 to the services at Junction Thirty. There was an impressive selection of food outlets providing a wide variety of choice if your key nutritional requirements were fat and sugar, a winning formula, judging by the popularity of Cardiff Gate as a destination. In fact, this Welcome Break facility appeared to have developed into a culinary Las Vegas, an oasis of indulgence in a desert of fruit and vegetables, that pulled in so many punters it was proving almost impossible for Derek to find somewhere to park.

Eventually spotting an available place on the other side of row M, he stopped the Jag and put on the right indicator, waiting for a break in the traffic or another motorist to allow him to cross. Despite the clearest of signals about his intentions, a small Peugeot chose to blatantly contravene the drivers' code: approaching from the opposite direction, the car slowed briefly and swung into the middle before turning sharply left into their space; the young man behind the wheel avoided eye contact but not smirking. Without hesitation, Sandra opened the glove compartment and took out a pen and paper; without consultation, Derek read out the offending number plate. They parked in the far corner by the coaches (Trips4Chips, Cake Escapes, The Butty Bus, PizzaStreaka, Burger Herder, Team Cream) and while Mrs Tile walked Benson, her husband phoned a contact at the DVLA. 'Greetings colleague Colin, Derek Tile here... I am this week but looking forward to Monday's presentation on the roundabout renaissance... wondering if you could run a reg number through the system...'

The two folding chairs were positioned at the top of a steep slope that provided an excellent vantage point from which to observe the proceedings below. Sandra was listening with interest as her husband set the scene. 'This is a police matter now. According to my information the vehicle is legal, but the registered keeper is Tony Gove, a nineteen-year-old male currently disqualified for drug driving. In March the aforementioned individual received a DR80 conviction and a twelve-month ban.'

'Driving while disqualified, that's a serious offence.'

'It could be prison time for Tony. What are the sandwich choices?'

She opened the Tupperware pot. 'Cheese and tomato or tuna and cucumber.'

'One of each, please... it seems Mr Gove is well known to our friends in the local constabulary. His career warrants a custodial sentence. He has to be driving, that's the important thing. Which is why they haven't clamped the vehicle, I imagine.'

Sandra sighed. 'All this over a parking place.'

'A connection exists, my love. There's a continuum of criminality. It's a small step from littering to maiming, from tailgater to sex trafficker.' They both ate in silence for a moment. 'Do we have any crisps?'

'Salt and vinegar. Anything happening down there?'

Derek surveyed the car park with binoculars. 'I can see the Peugeot in row M. Not much else at… hang on, there's a police vehicle near the motorway exit. That wasn't there a minute ago. They're setting a trap.'

'Can I have a go with them?' Sandra dangled the packet. 'Swap you.'

'It's an arrestable offence so Tony will be charged immediately. Of course, there's always a chance he hasn't come here just to buy petrol and *The Daily Telegraph*.'

'Someone's walking back to the car; I think it's the same person.' She adjusted the focus. 'He's carrying a brown bag.'

'That could be drugs. There's been an exchange.'

'No, it's a pasty. He's taken a bite.'

Mr Tile twitched. 'Maybe I should have a look.'

'It's my turn. You've got the crisps.'

'I think it would be best if I was in charge of the binoculars.'

'He's getting into the car.'

Derek's left arm reached over to snatch the field glasses; just in time, his right hand caught it by the wrist. He slapped his face. 'Don't do that. Sorry.' He slapped his face again. 'Don't do that. Sorry.' Slap. 'Don't do that. Sorry.' Slap. 'Don't do—'

'*Stop!*' She counted to five. He stared straight ahead, motionless. 'Here you are, you take them. I'll pour some coffee. Tell me what's going on.'

'Thank you, my love… the Peugeot's moving; nobody's following at this point… he's leaving the car park.'

'What are the police doing?'

'There's a vehicle wating on the slip road.' Derek frowned and readjusted the focus. 'It's unmarked but I think… yes, they're making a move. Time for the interception.'

'I can see. It's a pincer movement.'

'Four officers on the scene… it's looking lonely for Tony.'

Sandra handed him a cup. 'Bourbon biscuit with it?'

He glanced at her in surprise. 'Excellent idea, Mrs Tile.'

'I think it's allowed,' she smiled indulgently, 'we are on holiday, after all.'

An hour and thirty-four minutes later, they drove through the village of Burricon on the Gower Peninsula, following the narrow road as it twisted along the valley in search of the coast. Round a sharp bend there were signs for the beach, a large car park, cosy-looking pub, shop selling seaside essentials and a scattering of houses; half a mile further on, the track for the Burricon Bay Hotel appeared on the left by a copse of pine trees. The Jag turned towards its destination.

Originally built as a holiday home for a wealthy Swansea family in the 1920s, the property was requisitioned by the MOD in 1942, before falling into disrepair for nearly two decades. The abandoned complex briefly flourished as a hippy commune known as CALL (Centre for Alternative Languid Lifestyles) during the 1960s; founded by the errant son of a racehorse trainer, it developed into a cultural happening dedicated to weaving, LSD, pornographic musical theatre, upholstery, cider-pressing, genital art and the cultivation of crops, particularly root vegetables, by pre-industrial methods. This socio-agrarian experiment came to a dramatic end after the discovery that all manual labour on the farm was carried out, quite slowly, by what one tabloid referred to as a "slave class" of drugged, disorientated ex-jockeys stabled in the old army barracks. The resulting scandal enabled an enterprising local couple to purchase the house and land for a nominal sum, sympathetically restore, convert and extend the buildings, landscape the grounds, then open as a hotel in the late 1970s. Despite this, the legacy of CALL lived on in unexpected ways: documenting thirty years from 1985 to 2015, a demographic study by the ONS consistently recorded the UK's lowest average height among the population of the Gower Peninsula.

Mr Tile recounted this historical synopsis to his wife as they motored at a leisurely pace towards their home for the next five nights, before parking temporarily outside the main entrance. They had rented a cottage in the area earlier that year and trialled the establishment for lunch after a walk on the beach; not only did the food and service prove acceptable, but it also turned out the Burricon Bay Hotel offered dog-friendly accommodation in the form of ten static caravans situated within their own private meadow overlooking the sea. Half board provided breakfast and dinner in the restaurant with all the benefits and privacy of their own living space. Derek had been a canny winner about timing too: the June Special gave them five nights for the price of four and, by arranging their stay to coincide with his quarterly meeting at the DVLA in Swansea at 09:00 on Monday morning, he was entitled to claim for Sunday night's accommodation from the DfT. In real terms, he'd almost doubled their money, an impressive achievement that hadn't received quite the rapturous reception he'd envisaged when announcing the booking to Sandra. Apparently, a genuine surprise would be two weeks in a villa with a pool on Capri, not five nights in a Welsh caravan with the dog on a bargain break.

The receptionist greeted them cheerfully. 'Good afternoon, welcome to Burricon Bay. My name is Gwyn. Do you have a reservation?'

'Greetings, Gwyneth. We most certainly do, in the name of Tile.' Derek reached into his coat pocket. 'I have the confirmation here.'

She tapped on the keyboard. 'I can't see anything under Tiling.'

'Tile.'

'Oh, *Tile*. With one syllable. Like Gwyn.' She smiled innocently. 'Yes, here it is. Five nights in one of our lovely static homes. You'll be in Number Three.'

'Three? There must be a mistake. I specifically requested Number Ten when I spoke to your colleague.' He frowned. 'With good reason – it's at the end of the row, thus affording a greater degree of privacy when utilising the outside seating area.'

'I understand, Mr Tile, let me have a quick look.' Gwyn scrutinised the screen in front of her. 'I see you've taken advantage of our June Special...'

'We have.'

'That explains it then. Number Ten's not available with the offer. Now, can I interest you in any of our accommodation extras?'

'I don't think we'll be rushing—'

'That sounds interesting,' Sandra interrupted. 'What have you got, Gwyn?'

'Very popular with our couples is the luxury chocolate selection with a chilled bottle of Prosecco or champagne on ice. Brought to your accommodation whenever you choose.'

Derek shook his head. 'No, thank you—'

'We'll take the chocolates with champagne right away please. Just add it to the bill.'

A look of mutual understanding was exchanged between the two women. 'That order's been placed for you, Mrs Tile... I think you might be in luck. Number Ten isn't booked till next week. Would you like them sent there?'

With perfect timing, the delivery had arrived just as Sandra finished unpacking. In direct causal relationship to this event, she was lying on the caravan sofa at that precise moment, soaking in the sea view through the end windows. In one hand she held a glass of bubbly, in the other her third chocolate; by her feet, Benson munched happily on the complimentary dog biscuits thoughtfully included. The tranquil scene was interrupted by Derek's entrance through the outside door, brandishing a clipboard. 'Internal and external facilities check complete, together with full photographic inventory. One more thing to accomplish before we embark on a walk. If you don't mind, your presence is required in the bedroom for that, my love.'

His wife sipped her drink and looked at him. 'I see. Have you got something planned?'

'All will be revealed.'

She smiled and put her glass down. 'Well, you're certainly in the holiday mood.'

He was lying on the bed with one of her chiffon scarves tied round his head when Sandra came into the room. 'There's a fire,' Derek announced.

She closed the door. 'This sounds like a role play. Let me guess, I'm a paramedic and you're an injured fireman...'

'No, we're performing a simulation exercise.' He pulled the scarf over his eyes. 'It's the middle of the night when the smoke alarm goes off. That explains my current location. The purpose of the blindfold is to replicate minimal visibility inside the caravan. To make the training conditions realistic there can be no assistance of any kind. We must be prepared for an emergency situation in an unfamiliar environment. A fire could happen this very evening. Any questions?' There was a long silence. 'Are you still there?'

'This is what you disturbed me for?'

He pulled up the blindfold. 'Execution of the safety drill entails two participants working together. You're in charge of timing and observation. How long does it take me to get from this position to the NAP – Nominated Assembly Point? Does the exit route contain obstructions which need clearing? I'm putting my phone on stopwatch mode, all you have to do is press start when I give the signal.'

She strode over and tore the scarf off his head. 'Benson and I are going for a walk. We're leaving in ten minutes.' Mrs Tile paused in the doorway. 'Don't start wearing my clothes – that really would be the final straw.'

Since it was already 16:00, and they would be spending the day on the beach tomorrow, Sandra suggested following a route she'd found in the VIP (Visitor Information Pack) that took them through some woods to Rhos Cove, a small inlet round the headland. With an exertion rating of gentle to moderate, and a duration estimate of an hour and a half, it sounded like the perfect leg-stretcher after a lengthy car journey. Her husband (wisely) agreed.

They took the back gate out of the meadow and joined a footpath bisecting an open field until it reached the first of two stiles mentioned in the instructions; a left turn ran down the side of a fence towards the second. The track narrowed afterwards, and they walked in single file through a tunnel of overhanging hedgerows, emerging at the other end onto the coast path with its sudden spectacle of sea and sky.

Just ahead of him, Sandra froze mid-step. At first, Derek thought she was transfixed by the view, but she held her arm out behind, then beckoned slowly with her hand. Edging forward, he saw what merited such reverence: a few feet in front, a bold, brown hare sat in the middle of the trail facing them, its long front legs giving a markedly upright posture, the black-tipped ears straining like sails in the wind; a pair of amber eyes regarded them, unperturbed.

On this patch of grass at the edge of the peninsula, Lepus europaeus and Homo tileus considered each other, communed, as Sandra came to think of it later, in the stillness of the afternoon sun; unfortunately, the spell was broken by the belated appearance of Canis familiaris behind them. In one movement, the hare turned, sprang and vanished before Benson even noticed it was there.

'Remarkable,' Derek commented. 'They're normally extremely wary of people.'

His wife didn't move. 'Did you feel something happen then?'

'In what way?'

'That creature came to tell us something.'

He nodded. 'Could be. It was certainly strange. Preternatural even.'

'To be honest, I didn't really want to visit the Gower again on this holiday. But now, I think there's a reason.'

'Go on.'

Sandra turned round to face him. 'We're here to do something. I don't know what it is yet.' She paused. 'The hare does though. There's a plan that we're part of; it's why we've come.'

As he rounded the bend on the track above the bouldered beach of the promontory, leaving the wide sweep of Culvermead Bay behind, Leonard's mood was unsettled. Recently, he'd intuited that a change was taking place, almost imperceptibly, on the edge of his awareness; that he'd entered a liminal phase and was transiting an unfamiliar borderland like a passenger on a train.

Être sur le point de. For some reason, he remembered that rudimentary construction from secondary school. It was doubtful he'd thought of the phrase in decades, so why had it jumped into his head now? It felt like something was about to happen; he was on the verge of it but had no clear idea when or how this event would occur. Leonard sensed what was coming but its shape remained amorphous, out of focus, like a ship emerging through fog or a sculpture from stone. He wondered if, somewhere in the recesses of his mind, the answer lay dormant, like those five words of schoolboy French he'd filed away, waiting for translation.

Blocking the way ahead was a metal fence; in the middle of the panel hung a yellow sign with black writing:

PATH CLOSED

DUE TO COASTAL EROSION
THE CLIFFTOP PATH IS NOW CLOSED
UNTIL FURTHER NOTICE

The track turned inland and ran uphill, reaching a wood at the top of the incline where the sunbeams were sieved through the leaf canopy into countless flecks of powdered light. The only sound floating on the currents of warm air was the distant bark of a dog deep in the trees.

Mrs Tile stopped and listened. Fearing the worst, she called to her husband up ahead. '*Derek! where's Benson?*'

He looked around him, conscientiously, and marched back towards her. 'Not with you?'

This didn't warrant a response. She concentrated on the barking – it was to their right, a long way off. 'That direction,' she pointed. 'He's over there.'

Derek produced a PAN (Pro Altitude Navigator) orienteering compass – waterproof up to ten metres – from the inner compartment of his warm-weather, adventure gilet's front zip pocket. 'South-south-west. I've locked the direction. We're good to go. In the circumstances, I will assume field command and overall tactical control of the retrieval mission.'

'No, you won't.' She headed away from the track. '*Benson!*'

Reluctantly, he followed. After ten minutes of stumbling over roots, battling through undergrowth and brushing away branches, Mr Tile noticed that his wife had deviated from the course indicated on his compass by a considerable margin. '*Sandra!*'

'*What?*'

'*This way!*' he yelled.

'*No! Over here!*'

She was mistaken, obviously, but there would be no gloating when he brought the dog back safely to her; that would be unfair – he had the PAN advantage, after all. Much better to show grace in victory. In order to be fully prepared, Derek practised the expression of magnanimity he would maintain throughout the emotional reunion. He smiled quietly to himself, then tripped noisily over a stump.

There was good news and bad news as far as Sandra was concerned: the good, the last bark she'd heard had been close by; the bad, it had been a while ago. The woods had gone worryingly quiet ever since. She took a deep breath and tried again. '*Benson!*'

There was a brief pause, then a male (human) voice replied, '*Hello?*'

'*Hello!*'

'*Keep going... I can see you... he's with me.*'

In front of her stood an imposing figure, well over six feet and heavily muscled. His biker's beard was patterned with grey whorls that seemed to coil simultaneously up into the long hair tied in a ponytail and down into the faded tattoos traversing his arms. He held a stick by his side. Behind him, under a beech tree, was a tent; next to that lay Benson, eating. The man looked over at him. 'Likes carrots, doesn't he?'

'One of his favourites.'

They both listened to the sound of enthusiastic crunching. 'I've made some tea, if you want some.'

'Thank you.' She smiled.

'Have a seat on my new sofa.' He indicated a log by the firepit. 'I've gone for a rustic look in this room.'

'I like what you've done with it... I'm Sandra by the way.'

'Barry.' He nodded. 'And that's Benson, is it? He found me here. Wouldn't shut up till I gave him some food.' Barry chuckled. 'Have you believe he's half-starved. Milk and sugar?'

'A bit of each please.' As she stroked the dog, Sandra realised there was a clear view through the trees to a small inlet just below – Rhos Cove, the destination of their walk. In the open water beyond the bay, a small outcrop – marked on the map as the Mew Stone – jutted out of the sea. 'Not a bad spot.'

'Been here a few days. Longer than intended, as it happens. I twisted my ankle; that set me back a bit. I like to keep moving. Also, word gets about.'

'Does it?'

'Give it a week, and all of this,' Barry slowly swept his forearm in a wide arc as if encompassing the Great Plains, 'will be a campsite. With the attendant grief.' He raised his substantial eyebrows which, once aloft, appeared to hover semi-autonomously. 'Now, last time I checked, I didn't have a licence for camping. Therefore, the presence of motorhomes and shower blocks on this land would imperil my liberty.' He flicked his stick like the tail of an irritated cat then threw it on the ground. 'And that is a very serious matter.'

'Of course.'

'Besides,' he handed her a mug, 'I'm on my way to Ireland. Got some festival work coming up.'

'Are you walking there?'

'That's the plan. I left Southampton in January.' He chuckled again. 'Need to get a move on, don't I?'

Sandra smiled. 'What's the rush?'

'None really.' They both drank their tea in silence for a minute. 'It's nice talking to someone. Only thing I miss, as it happens. Been keeping a diary instead, stops me talking to myself.' He looked at her and seemed to be making a decision. 'It's not just where I've been and what happened. Do you want to hear a bit?'

'I do.'

Barry got up and disappeared into the tent, returning moments later with a thick notebook. He opened it near the end and found the right page. 'I wrote this yesterday. It's called "The Traveller":

'A traveller wandered miles searching for the secret of happiness.

He found a woman by a river playing the harp. He asked her which way to go. "Swim across to the other side and walk through the woods. Beyond them you will find the secret of happiness."

He swam the river and went through the woods.

There was nothing there. She had lied.

Many miles further on the traveller passed two children singing. He asked them which way to go. "Climb to the top of that far mountain and you will find a lake which holds the secret of happiness." He climbed to the very top.

There was no lake. They had lied.

Further still the traveller wandered. He came to a man standing at a crossroads. He asked him which way to go. The man turned and punched the cunt hard in the face, the fist smashing his teeth like a brick. The traveller dropped, cracking open his skull on a rock.

There were no more questions.'

Barry closed the book. As Sandra was about to speak, he held up his hand. 'No need to say anything. I just wanted someone to hear it.'

'Thank you for sharing the poem. I enjoyed it.'

He stared at the ground, then looked up suddenly with a wide grin. 'Do you want to come to Ireland with me? I wouldn't mind that. We could leave now, if you like.'

Sandra burst out laughing. 'Your tent doesn't look very big, Barry, and I'm a married woman.' In the bay below, she caught sight of somebody standing on the thin strip of beach waving an object towards the sea; the course south-south-west appeared to have encountered a small problem. She sighed. 'It's tempting, believe me, but I think my festival days are over.'

When she reached the bottom of the slope where the shingle started, Mrs Tile ducked behind a bush. She watched her husband pacing in small circles, his arm rhythmically jerking up and down with the compass, like an escaped figure from a giant automaton clock. She let Benson run onto the beach and scurried round the back of the trees, emerging at the other end of the cove a few minutes later.

Derek saw her approach and jumped about, waving exultantly, then picked up the dog and held him aloft like a trophy. As Sandra got nearer, his expression abruptly changed – as if he remembered something – from one of triumph to a peculiar kind of grimace/leer combination; she wondered if he was getting constipated again.

FIVE

They were on the outdoor terrace of the hotel restaurant at 17:32 immersed in TCP (Table Choice Ponderation). The place didn't officially open for another twenty-eight minutes, but an agreeable waiter named Will had allowed them access to consider their options, meaning they were enjoying a private view before the general public arrived. Nine minutes later, with rare unanimity, the Tiles had agreed on a shortlist.

In many ways, this next stage represented a greater challenge, as Derek knew from his (brief) experience of interviewing job applicants at work, prior to his removal from the selection panel for asking questions deemed irrelevant to the advertised role of Data Security Analyst. (An example quoted in his review was: "what long-term benefits would targeted sterilisation in agricultural communities produce?".) Having got this far, the candidates all had much to recommend them. Consequently, the process involved a second and sometimes third round of assessment before a final decision was reached.

By 17:51, having revisited each shortlisted table at least once and discussed their individual merits in considerable detail, it had come down to a choice of two. Unfortunately, neither Tile was keen to express a decisive preference and thus potentially be held responsible for a mistake. The debate might have lasted all night if Will hadn't arrived, glancing at his watch. 'Have we got a winner?'

Sandra made a face. 'Nearly. It's between the two at the end on the front row.'

The waiter nodded. 'They always go first. I'd take the one on the right. It's got a better line of sight into the restaurant, meaning you won't get forgotten.'

'Excellent insight, William. Refreshingly competent. I think we've found the perfect table, my love.' Derek beamed with satisfaction as they secured dinner and breakfast reservations for the duration of their stay: ten meals without any cooking or the need for TCP; fifteen, if you included picnic lunches provided courtesy of the morning buffet. All in all, the holiday had started rather well.

Back at the caravan, Mr Tile showered first, then changed for dinner, before vacating the premises as requested while his wife got ready. Knowing there was a half-hour window of opportunity, he considered a quiet drink, contemplating the sea and the vanity of human endeavour, perhaps with some peanuts, to be fully justified. On his way through the kitchen, he took a bottle of Newcastle Brown out of the fridge and went outside; relaxing on the bench, he took a long swig of cold ale in the balmy June evening. For a while he could feel himself floating out on the water, weightless in the current, dopamine glinting in his brain like sunlight.

It felt like they'd been there for a week already, not part of one afternoon, a phenomenon he recognised as contextual familiarisation. In his (unparalleled) experience, CONFAM occurred at its most striking on the first day of a beach holiday, particularly if you were lucky enough to be experiencing some winter sun. One minute you're trudging to work in the dark, hunched against the January misery, feeling your actual bones are cold and tired; the next, you're stepping onto the warm sands of languorous undress, joining a fiesta of fleshly devotion, a carnival of corporeal relish, as if you'd wandered into the extras' holding area for an al fresco adult-content shoot. But this was the strange thing: within a few hours, it seemed perfectly normal that everyone was pretty much naked; although it would be fundamentally dishonest to claim he hardly noticed his surroundings, the novelty wore off remarkably quickly.

He became aware of Sandra standing in the doorway, watching him. 'Everything alright, my love?'

'You tell me. Why have you got that look on your face?'

'What look?'

She thought about this. 'If I didn't know better, I'd say it was lechery.'

'That dress suits you.' His eyes twinkled. 'How long have we got before supper?'

She laughed and shook her head. 'No chance. You missed your moment earlier. I'm all clean and shiny now.'

The Tiles enjoyed a very pleasant meal at their table, looked after attentively by Will, whom they got into conversation with when he brought out the coffee. 'Thank you.' Sandra smiled. 'Have you been working here long?'

'Only a week so far this year. But I did the season last summer, so I know most of the staff.'

'Aha.' Derek nodded. 'What are you studying?'

The waiter hesitated a moment. 'I'm doing a master's in forensic science.' He looked round the restaurant to check if there was time for a chat. 'It's what I've wanted to do since I was fourteen.'

'How unusual,' Sandra commented.

'Better wear my driving gloves tomorrow night,' Derek commented.

'The house where I grew up was quite isolated,' Will continued, 'and one night we got broken into. The scary thing was, all of us were upstairs asleep. None of us heard anything. It was awful coming down the next morning and realising you'd been burgled, that someone had come in and ransacked your home. Anyway, this forensic scientist came to investigate; I was fascinated by everything she did. Then, a couple of days later, we got a phone call from the police saying they'd made an arrest based on fingerprint evidence found at the scene. It felt really good to know someone had been caught. From that moment, it was what I wanted to do.'

The Tiles looked at each other. 'Interesting story,' he observed.

'How did they break in and ransack the place without waking you up?' she asked.

'Somewhat far-fetched,' he agreed.

The waiter was incredulous. 'I don't know, it's what happened… sorry, you don't believe me?'

'Sounds more like an inside job, William.'

There was silence for a few moments. 'Damn. Needs some work then.' Will grinned. 'I'm creating the backstory for a character I'm playing. He's a forensic scientist. To answer your original question, Mr Tile, I'm studying drama.'

*

Appearing on a chat show ten years later to promote his new film, the period romance *Jane Austen's Corset*, the actor William Tile (born William Shatner. His parents were *Star Trek* fans) would relate this story about the origin of his stage name with great fondness, regarding it as a salutary early lesson in never underestimating your audience, even if there are only two of them. Keeping a sense of perspective sometimes proved difficult in the glamorous world of showbusiness, the celebrity guest would caution, especially if you achieved success at a young age; his chosen alias helped him stay grounded. Not everyone would agree with this assessment.

*

There were in fact three reasons Derek suggested a digestif to his wife:

1. It was the first night of their holiday and he felt foolhardy.
2. A recent diktat by the Ministry of Health had licensed spirits for special occasions only. Opportunities needed to be taken.
3. The budding thespian was showing little inclination to resume his current duties in the restaurant, being far more interested in feedback on his performance.

'Nice-looking boy, I'm sure he'll go far,' she predicted when the waiter (finally) left.

'I'm afraid that will largely be a matter of luck. Unlike my success in courting you, my love.'

After dinner, they strolled slowly round the grounds of the property, lingering in the gardens where the scent of pine permeated the summer dusk and the only sound was the wash of waves on the fading beach beneath them. Sandra felt him take her hand and squeeze it gently; neither felt the need for anything else.

As the perimeter path was becoming difficult to follow in the darkness, and the temperature had dropped significantly in the last half-hour, they decided to head back to the light and warmth of their new abode. It had been a long day and tiredness had finally caught up with them down the M4.

The first indication of a problem was the faint rhythmic thump they heard on the other side of the hotel. At the turning for the access road to the meadow they stopped, listening with hare-like intensity. Its precise locus was difficult to gauge; given the stillness of the evening, any loud music would be likely to travel a significant distance; it could conceivably be coming from somewhere inside the main building. They walked on, pausing as they approached the site entrance, their heads swivelling like satellite dishes locating a signal. It became inescapable that the source of the noise pollution was one of the static homes.

Mrs Tile succinctly summarised the situation. 'Oh dear.'

Her husband checked his watch. 'The regulations clearly state that no music is to be played after ten o'clock, out of consideration for other guests. It is now eleven minutes past.'

'Let's not worry about it yet; everyone's on holiday… the question is, how close are they?'

Unfortunately, the answer was next door. The nearer they got, the louder it became. The volume increased with each caravan number; they rose in conjunction. A terrible truth dawned on them as they progressed up the scale towards Ten: while they were out enjoying a quiet meal, new neighbours had moved in; neighbours who now appeared to be staging their own private festival. And those days were definitely over for Sandra. 'We'll give them till half-past. That's not unreasonable.'

Taking Benson out provided the perfect opportunity for Derek to engage in some preliminary reconnaissance. He walked down the side of their pitch and joined a track that ran along the site's edge in front of the static homes, enabling him to hide in the shadows while carrying out observation and appraisal of the new arrivals. With the curtains open and all the lights on, the large end windows gave the neighbours' living room the appearance of a glass showcase containing a moving diorama, set to a raucous soundtrack. The title of the exhibit on display was *The Night of The Mauling*.

A man and woman in their thirties were partying, singing and dancing next to a table laden with an impressive quantity of booze; a boy of about ten, naked apart from his socks and a superhero cape, was trampolining frenetically between sofas; and a small child was lying on the floor screaming, yanking the ear of a dog next to it. Not just any dog but an egregious example of a TUP (Totally Unsuitable Pet). This monster was a nightmarish pit bull-Rottweiler-hyena cross, the kind of beast bred to guard salvage yards, not play with young children. If this family were the neighbours from hell, they'd brought Cerberus with them on holiday. Unnoticed by either adult, the hound of Hades was staring at the toddler's head with a thoughtful expression, as if considering whether to rip the throat out first or get straight to work disfiguring its face. Derek had seen enough; he was not looking forward to asking them to turn the music down. 'The only thing that canine should play with is a landmine,' he informed Benson as they walked back.

Sandra looked up from a magazine. 'Have you been there yet?'

'I tried. There was no answer.' He started taking off his coat. 'Do you want some herbal tea?'

'You didn't go, did you?'

'No. I decided it would be wise not to take him with me. Their dog doesn't look very friendly.'

'The music probably wouldn't be a problem in Number Three. Where we were originally allocated. But we seem to have found ourselves in Number Ten, right next door. Where it is.' She put the magazine down. 'Don't tell me I have to go round?'

He racked his brain for a cogent reason. 'Would that be more effective, do you think?' Her stare indicated they would never find out. 'I'm going. Right now.'

'Good luck.' She carried on reading.

Mr Tile practised a friendly yet firm expression on the way over to the neighbours' caravan and banged on the door. There was no answer. He waited, bitterly regretting wasting the excuse. Nothing. He banged again, harder. Cue ferocious barking from three heads, then a man shouting,

'*Shut it JJ!*' The door opened slightly. 'Who's there?'

Before he could reply, a woman's voice yelled, '*Who is it, Lee?*'

'*I don't know!*'

Derek tried to make contact. 'Hello...'

As soon as he spoke, the barking resumed. He heard the woman again. '*What do they want?*'

'*I don't fucking know!*' Lee screamed.

'*Tell them to get lost!*'

'Who is it?' Lee asked, through the crack.

'Greetings, my name is Derek...'

'Who?' At this moment, the woman shouted something inaudible. '*What? Kay! Turn it down!*'

'*Lee!*'

The dog started barking again. '*Turn the fucking music down!*'

'*What's going on, Lee?*'

'*Kay!* Right, fuck this... hold on a minute.' Lee shut the door. There was a heated exchange, then the music stopped. A few moments later, the door opened a fraction again. 'You still there?'

'Yes.'

Lee waited. 'Go on then, what is it?'

Derek couldn't think of anything. 'Breakfast... do you know when it is?'

'In the morning, generally.'

'Any idea what time?'

Lee considered the question. 'Depends when we get up. Some days could be early, some days could be late... you from the hotel?'

'No. I'm in the caravan next door to you.'

Lee's head appeared. 'What's it got to do with you when we have breakfast?'

'No, I wasn't asking that.'

'Why's that any of your business?'

'Sorry, I'm not making myself clear. What I was trying—'

'Boxers and a T-shirt.'

'Excuse me?'

'That's what I wear, since you're so interested.' There was an awkward pause and Lee peered forward. 'Are you accusing me of something?'

'What?'

'If you want to accuse me of something, then crack on.'

'I'm not.'

'Have you ever or have you not come here to make accusations?'

'No, I haven't.'

'Out of ten, how much evidence have you got?'

'None. I'm not suggesting I do.'

'Shouldn't be making accusations then. That puts you on dangerous ground. Imagine I come round to your place with no evidence and claim you stole my shelving unit… not a nice feeling, is it?'

The conversation seemed to be spinning out of control; unclear how they'd got there, Derek attempted a reset. 'There appears to be some confusion about what—'

'Seriously, I don't mind. Fill your boots. Makes no difference to me. It will have to be proved, but you crack on.'

'I'm not accusing you of anything.'

'No comment.'

'Sorry?'

'No comment.' Lee folded his arms. 'I have no further comment to make during this interview.'

'I'm not from the police.'

'Because if you want to accuse me of something, I want it proved. Either way, innocent or guilty, it needs to be proved. What you'll find is, I'm answering no comment from now on.'

Derek heard the woman's voice in the background. 'You done yet?'

Lee turned round. 'Kay, come here a minute.'

'I can't roll a spliff, have a drink, babysit *and* talk to someone over there, Lee.'

'Yes or no, do we want a shelving unit?'

'Not right now, no.'

'What time's breakfast tomorrow?'

'When someone makes it. Why?'

'The bloke next door wants to come over.'

There was a short silence. 'He does, does he?'

Derek tried to extricate himself. 'No. Look, you've misunderstood...'

'I don't think so.' Lee winked at him. 'You came here to have a go about the music, didn't you? Now you're a bit fucked.'

Kay put her head round the door. 'Evening. Would it be convenient if I took your order now, sir? We're serving a full English tomorrow, that's bacon, eggs and all the works. What about a handjob after, on the house? Would eight o'clock suit you?' She glared at him. 'I've got two kids, this one and his dog to look after. It's not a fucking caff. You got that?'

Dumbstruck, Derek simply nodded. Kay withdrew inside and immediately the massive, black muzzle of the hellhound appeared, at exactly the same level as his crotch. It sniffed and licked its lips. Lee was grinning. 'That didn't go so well, did it? Don't think she likes you. Mind you, no one likes a nosy neighbour. I know JJ doesn't.' Encouraged by hearing its name, the dog's head pushed through the door; it was the size of a basketball. The livid eyes focused on the soft, exposed flesh of Derek's cheeks, ears and neck.

He backed away, slowly. 'Apologies for the disturbance.'

Lee hadn't quite finished. 'We live next door to this bloke at home. He used to be a nosy neighbour. JJ didn't like that. Killed his dog… sleep tight.'

As Derek opened the door to his caravan, the music came on again. Not as loud as before but loud enough. It lasted about twenty minutes, just to send a message, then abruptly stopped. And that's when Kay and Lee's argument started. Petty and point-scoring at first, it swiftly exploded into a sulphurous slanging match of abusive pyrotechnics.

With no breeze, the guttural cries of the trailer-dwelling howler monkeys travelled several miles through the Welsh forest; fifty feet away, with only thin aluminium panels for protection, the Tiles had little hope of escaping a nocturnal cacophony that continued long after midnight. Despite employing earplugs and Sandra's zopiclone, neither of them got to sleep until the early hours.

SIX

Mr Tile was woken by the noise of external activity. Feeling strangely groggy, he sat up slowly and peered through the bedroom window. On the upside, their neighbours were departing for a day on the beach. On the downside, they were leaving the dog behind, tied up by the caravan. As soon as the family disappeared from view, the animal started barking maniacally. His wife stirred and turned her face towards him. 'Be quiet, Derek,' she muttered and rolled over. A few moments passed and her patience appeared to run out: 'Shut up!' Either JJ didn't hear or chose to ignore the injunction. 'What time is it?'

'Morning, my love. It's just gone nine o'clock.'

She lifted her eye mask. 'Why is the dog barking like that?'

'They've gone out and left it.'

'Make it stop.' Sandra replaced the mask. 'Wake me in an hour.' Then she added, in a sign her cognitive and gastric functions were unaffected by the night's disturbance, 'I don't want to miss breakfast.'

He climbed wearily out of bed, put on the squirrel-red dressing gown from his spring/summer collection and plodded through to the kitchen, closing the door considerately but pointlessly behind him. At the end of a (reassuringly) thick rope, Beelzebub's pup was straining, snarling, leaping and baying wildly; there was absolutely no indication it would tire before the autumn. Derek watched from the living room, uncertain how to proceed.

Deciding that lying on the sofa might furnish him with inspiration, he turned round and walked straight into the edge of the coffee table; directly below his head, as he bent down to rub the afflicted shin, in the position where she'd left it the night before, sat the packet of Sandra's prescription sleeping pills. That explained the grogginess. He opened it – there were only two gone; she could spare a few more; after all, the point of them was to help her sleep. One way or another.

He lined up the zopiclone in a neat, equidistantly spaced row on the kitchen worktop and opened the fridge. Picking through the surprisingly large number of items inside, he discovered a Tupperware pot containing cooked chicken breasts. The commis chef selected the largest one, placed it on the chopping board and quartered the portion. Into each segment he cut a deep, narrow incision, pushed two tablets to the bottom of the crevice, then pinched the parcels of coq au sommeil together. That was the easy part. Despite the particular care he'd taken with placement, there remained a concern that just chucking the chicken pieces within JJ's reach might dislodge the magic ingredient in the dish; the last thing he wanted was to simply provide a tasty snack and more barking fuel. The food had to be presented to the customer, not by hand – a potentially life-threatening manoeuvre – but using a SAM (Specially Assembled Mechanism). A delivery device needed to be engineered; ever resourceful, Derek already had something in mind.

He collected the essential components from various drawers and cupboards in the kitchen environs, then established a workshop on the living room floor. Arranged in chronological order of requirement were: ruler, tape, scissors, coffee table, pink dustpan, broom and packet of custard cream biscuits. First, he measured and cut five strips of tape exactly ten inches long and hung them in turn from the edge of the table; next, the dustpan was offered up to the non-brush end of the broom and, once he was satisfied with the positioning, secured in place with tape; then, with the biscuit packet substituting for bait in the dustpan, SAM underwent rigorous field testing for reach and stability; finally, the custard creams were opened and two consumed while he admired his handiwork. Benson looked over, stretched and dragged himself out of bed, motivated purely by affection.

Outside the caravan, Derek arranged the narco-chicken chunks neatly in the pink, plastic skillet, presentation being important in both the restaurant and drug trades, lifted SAM to operational height and proceeded round the corner. When the irate canine caught sight of Mr Tile approaching, it momentarily stopped barking out of sheer astonishment, the huge head tilting slightly to one side. (Tableau: ageing, bearded man wearing red dressing gown and all-terrain, sport sandals, attempts to propitiate monstrous dog-demon, equipped only with homemade broomstick/dustpan contraption and paltry poultry offering.) The hiatus didn't last long. Rushing forward, the creature sprang at his throat, immediately being yanked back by the limit of the rope and smacking to the ground. With it coughing violently, he seized the chance to advance as close as possible, laying SAM temptingly between them. JJ stopped, sniffed and scoffed the starter in four seconds flat, then looked up to appraise the main course; Derek made a prompt tactical withdrawal, turning round in time to glimpse the black ponytail and yellow jacket of a jogger disappearing down the path. The barking resumed at full volume.

In the caravan, Sandra had given up trying to sleep and started her morning ablutions; Benson was waiting patiently for her by the door with his lead. When the two of them returned from a walk in the adjacent field, the three of them went for breakfast in the restaurant. Mrs Tile chose fruit, croissant and yoghurt from the extensive selection available; against Health Ministry advice, her husband opted for a full English with bacon, eggs and all the works, as he put it. While Derek was finishing his coffee at their table, she took the opportunity to reallocate some rolls, cheese and cold meats from the buffet to a lunchtime picnic on the beach; with perfect timing, the sun had started to come out.

It was after they got back from breakfast that Mr Tile decided to kill the dog. Or, more accurately, he couldn't think of a good reason not to. The idea of canicide crossed his mind by chance, came into view suddenly, like one of those red kites he sometimes saw at home; it circled on the thermals of possibility, then flew down and landed on the lawn. The notion became unignorable.

Walking up the meadow past the row of static homes, Sandra held out her arm to stop him. 'Listen... nothing! Just exquisite silence.' They rounded the end of Number Nine and caught sight of the creature lying on its side, motionless, a black form the size of a Shetland pony. She smiled, raised her eyebrows and took Benson to the caravan.

Derek approached the inert body and gave it a tentative poke from behind. No reaction. He prodded a bit harder, ready to run if need be. It didn't move. The thing was comatose, utterly insensate; Doctor Zop had done his job. That's when the thought occurred to him. Why not? The Tile code of conduct sanctioned the use of any solution proportionate to the problem under MOB (Maintaining Orderly Balance) rule 4C Part II. If ever there was an occasion that justified, demanded even, direct intervention of an irrevocable kind, this was it. Fate had provided the motive and opportunity; the Jag's boot and a kitchen cupboard would supply the means. No question, it was for the greater good.

He unlocked the car and got the two bungees needed, then went to find the bin liners he'd spotted earlier in the caravan. Sandra was sitting on the sofa, occupied with her phone. She looked up. 'What are you doing?'

'Just finishing something off, my love.'

'OK. I'm going to speak to my sister about tomorrow while you're doing that. I hope you haven't forgotten we're having lunch with them.'

The plan was simple: secure the animal's front legs with one bungee and tie the plastic bag over its head with the other; it would all be over quite fast, without undue suffering. JJ was a dog after all, and Derek liked dogs.

Just to make sure, he gave it another nudge in the back with SAM – nothing – then walked round the front. Bending down to perform the first part of the operation, he noticed something strange: its eyes were open. They had a vacant look, as if watching daytime television, and the pupils were markedly dilated. Utilising a nugget of information that he'd picked up on the RLSS (UK) Lifeguard course, Derek tapped the corner of an eye. It didn't blink.

When he'd taken Ben to be euthanised nine years before – one of the top five most distressing experiences of his entire life – the young, spotty vet had checked for a pulse after administering the lethal injection. He placed two fingers on Ben's chest near the elbow joint, then explained, unnecessarily and rather matter-of-factly as Derek recalled (perhaps not unrelated to an earlier enquiry about the extent of his experience), how the heart would gradually slow until it stopped beating altogether. Derek repeated the procedure now; there was no pulse. Without any doubt whatsoever, the dog was already dead. He gathered everything up and went to report this interesting turn of events to his wife.

'How many zopiclone did you give it?'

'Eight. Which shouldn't be enough to kill an animal that size.'

There was the hint of a smile on her lips. 'It obviously was.'

'Not without an unusual allergic reaction. Or pre-existing condition. Neither could have been foreseen.'

'I'm sure your friend Lee will be pleased to hear the drug overdose wasn't meant to kill his dog. That was a mistake. It was supposed to be suffocation.'

Derek hadn't actually considered Lee's reaction before. He did now. 'Do you think we should leave?'

'There's no need. Nothing's happened. We'll go to the beach, as planned. The dog was in rude health when we last saw it. Now, why don't you get everything ready while I make the picnic?'

After not much consideration, Derek agreed that nothing was in fact what did happen and therefore ignorance of the dog's death would be entirely reasonable in the circumstances. It reminded him of a story in the book he was rereading, Cornelius Levering's 1884 classic *A Recommended History of Noteworthy Felonies in the County of Berkshire*, which recounted a terrible miscarriage of justice. On the evening of 17 March 1820, John Manklin, a woodworker, and Bob Cowper, an itinerant seasonal labourer, met in an alehouse outside the town of Newbury. They were planning a poaching trip, an activity in which Bob had considerable experience. Two nights later, the men convened as arranged on the land of Sir Henry Beynon; the weather couldn't have been worse for hunting – moonless and stormy – and in the darkness they quickly became separated. John returned home several hours later with a brace of pheasants for the pot, retired to bed and went to work as usual the next day. One week later, he was arrested on suspicion of grand larceny: stealing a horse from Sir Henry's estate on the night of 19 March; at the time, an offence which carried the death penalty.

Mary Barton, landlady of the tavern, had reported that she overheard Mr Manklin and another unknown man discussing their plan at some length on the seventeenth of that month. Faced with this testimony, John admitted trespass and the poaching of pheasants, crimes (only) punishable by whipping and the confiscation of property but denied any knowledge of horse theft. He maintained that he'd acted alone, and his drinking companion had been merely a casual acquaintance. His version of events was not accepted by the court and John Manklin was hanged on a gibbet in Newbury town square *pour encourager les autres*. As George Savile, 1st Marquess of Halifax, put it two centuries earlier: "men are not hanged for stealing horses, but that horses may not be stolen". Three years too late for John, equine larceny ceased to be a capital offence under the reforming 1823 Judgement of Death Act.

Six months after his friend's public execution, Bob Cowper repaid him by marrying a recently widowed local beauty named Becky Manklin. Worse was to follow. On his deathbed in 1831, his lungs destroyed by tuberculosis, Bob confessed to selling a fine chestnut mare at Reading's May Fair eleven years before which he'd stolen from Henry Beynon. Continuing in this revelatory vein, he divulged that landlady Barton had received part of the sale proceeds in return for her selective account of that fateful evening to the justices. Mary had already passed beyond earthly judgement; Becky's innocence or guilt in the matter remained the subject of fervid speculation.

Mr Tile drew three main conclusions from this sorry tale:

1. Admit nothing. "Yet small confessions make great gallows", as Cornelius Levering noted.
2. Don't trust pub landladies who linger near your table without obvious reason, appearing to be friendly.

3. No good ever came of encountering a pheasant, as any
    motorist who has travelled down a country lane will testify.

When the expedition leader had scouted a suitable location
on the beach to make camp, she sat down on the soft sand
with Benson and waited for the bearded bearer to arrive
with the equipment. Bringing up the rear by some distance,
the long-term effects of LAD (Load Allocation Disparity),
combined with the shifting desert terrain, had taken a
considerable toll on Derek: fat beads of sweat like bubble
wrap covered his face and neck; the weight of bags welded
to his hands dragged arm muscle from bone by the tendon;
and knuckles of pain scaffolded his back from a rucksack
the size of a house. Other than that, he was enjoying the
outing.

'Not as fit as you were,' Mrs Tile observed when her
husband finally caught up, staggering like a giant, dying
beetle.

'Apologies, my love,' he panted. 'Entirely my fault, the
passing of time.'

His first job, after a brief water break, was to erect the
new beach shelter. One of the many appealing qualities of the
Sun Dome Outdoor Master Instant Shader (zippered porch
included) that justified its exorbitant price tag, according
to the helpful sales assistant in the camping shop, was the
pop-up design, facilitating quick and easy assembly. Half
an hour later, as he lay on the ground wrapped in polyester
sheeting and telescopic poles, Derek began to doubt the
veracity of that claim.

The construction site was a hard-nosed environment,
and following a bad-tempered appearance before the

employment tribunal, he found himself unceremoniously demoted and reassigned to lowly windbreak work. This less-challenging role proved significantly more successful, so much so that in less than ten minutes he had put up an attractive, U-shaped, canvas perimeter fence, slightly longer than it took Sandra to sort out the recalcitrant canopy.

As the project manager took charge of the tent's interior design, library services and pet department, the minimum-wage labourer embarked on the initial phase of his ambitious pre-lunch project: a scale-model recreation of the M25 from memory. Not only would the sand sculpture represent an impressive achievement in itself, but the finished piece would also provide a buffer zone against the perennial problem of CSIs (Contiguous Space Invaders). A less overt statement than a wall, area of ploughed-up no man's land or strategically placed satellite camps – all previously tried, with varying degrees of compliance – the art installation would provide aesthetic pleasure to the beachgoing public (all donations to the RLSS and Red Squirrel Survival Trust) as well as forming a subtle but inviolable barrier.

Once he'd drawn two concentric circles around the outside of the windbreak, taking care to achieve consistency of diameter, Derek marked out the access path to the inner sanctum. This channel would serve as the physical entrance, Junction 15 (M4) and due west. The hard work began with building the raised motorway – two shallow trenches needed to be excavated either side of the orbital route, the sand deposited in the middle and then levelled to form the road surface; in effect, it meant digging a double-ditch that circumnavigated Greater London with only a small spade. By any measure, this constituted an Olympian challenge of epic proportions, the stuff of Greek myth, meriting a mayoral speech in the town square, banners and garlands, local press, a squad of old women in black, traditional dancing and a presentation of flowers to the heroic Derikhos (accepted modestly), followed by meze platters at the family restaurant with keftedes, dolmades and all the works – washed down with retsina, toasted with ouzo – as fortification. Surprisingly, there were no cheering crowds or Hellenic tavernas on the Welsh beach, so he had to settle for a Penguin.

Mr Tile moved clockwise round the capital, deciding to position motorway junctions first, then fill in the A-roads, service stations and other details after lunch. An hour later, he had visited J16 (M40), J21 (M1), J23, A1(M) – debatable but just qualifying – J27 (M11), made the Dartford Crossing – technically part of the orbital route and certainly a landmark feature – between J31 in Essex and J1A in Kent, passed J3 (M20) and was now resting near Sevenoaks, having completed J5 (M26). By his calculations, roughly two-thirds of the initial stage had been completed; Derek felt rather proud and took some more pictures with his compact travel camera.

'What are you making?'

He looked round. A girl of about twelve was standing a few feet away in the county of Hertfordshire. 'It's a model.'

This seemed to come as something of a surprise. 'Really? Of what?'

'The M25. Do you know what that is?' She shook her head. 'Well,' he put the camera down and started explaining, 'it's a very big road that goes all the way—'

The girl was laughing. 'Of course I know what the M25 is, you halfwit.'

A few people had stopped to admire his efforts, so he'd grown accustomed to fielding questions; however, the arrival of this POC (Prodigiously Obnoxious Child) caught him off guard. 'Are your parents here or have they emigrated without you?'

'They're listening to Radio 4. I've got to explore the beach and draw what I find with words.' The girl studied him with interest, as if she was on safari. 'So far I've met a pensioner who has something of the fool about him.'

Derek glanced at the spade and momentarily considered adding bratricide to his list of misdemeanours that morning. He smiled instead. 'I suggest you go away now, before it's too late—'

'And can't even make sandcastles. He keeps trying but his attempts are dismal.' She seemed pleased with this sketch and wrote it down in a notebook from her bag. 'Yes, that's good... my name's Sarah-Jane. I'm being homeschooled until I'm older, then I'm going to Oxford. What's your name?' Foolishly (and yes, he reflected later, this was the appropriate adverb), he told her. 'Like the crane?'

'No. Sounds the same but spelt differently.' And then came the second mistake. 'Those words are called homophones.'

'*You* might spell it differently, but it *can* be spelt the same. Those words are called homonyms... look at me, I'm a crane called Derrick!' She held her arm straight out to the side with the hand dropped down and swung it back and forth. 'Hello, my name's Derrick, I'm a derrick!' She was *very* pleased with this and repeated it several times... 'Hello, I'm Derrick the derrick! Who are you? I'm a derrick called Derrick!' – segueing into a delighted playground taunt – 'Der-rick's a der-rick! Der-rick the der-rick!'

Judging the only way to avoid prison was ignoring the POC, he carried on with his project, crouching down where he'd left off at J5 (M26). The girl initially followed Mr Tile as he resumed moulding the masterwork, providing narration in the style of a wildlife documentary: 'The gormless castaway must adapt quickly to this new environment, or he will perish. There is much to learn. Not a skilled hunter, he is trying to catch fish in the sand. No luck this time. Robinson Clueless forages on the beach for food, storing any morsels in his beard...' Eventually, it all went quiet; when Derek peered over his shoulder to check, there was no sign of Sarah-Jane in the fields of Kent.

He spent the next fifteen minutes happily working his way round to J7 (M23), before starting to feel hungry. He was aware that some people (Sandra) would consider it to be marking your own homework, but in his not completely uninformed opinion, the Crawley/Brighton exit definitely had a certain architectural authority, a pleasing structural symmetry, the sort of competition-standard finesse which (at the very least) warranted its own dedicated photographic record. It wasn't until he reached the Thames Estuary that it dawned on him his camera had been stolen.

Mrs Tile was consuming a cheese and bacon roll; her husband was consumed by seething outrage. She passed him a Scotch egg. 'You left an expensive camera lying on the ground. Anyone could have picked it up when you were distracted. It's far from certain she took it.'

'I'm certain. You didn't meet her.'

'Can you not let it ruin the afternoon, please. Make an insurance claim when we get home. There's not much else you can do.'

'There is, my love. Benson and I can form a search party to sweep the beach. There will be no hiding place. The guarding Dobermanns and circling ravens will give Damienne away.'

Sandra sighed and opened a packet of Wotsits. 'If you find this girl by some miracle, and she's with her parents, then don't just accuse her in front of them. Give Sarah-Jane the chance to save face... you were showing her the camera because she was interested, and you think that possibly, by complete accident, she walked off with it.'

'That's not what happened.' He was in no mood to compromise. 'She stole somebody else's property. Mine, to be precise. There were no mitigating circumstances.'

Mrs Tile rolled her eyes. 'It doesn't matter. Do you want it back, or not? This gives her a get-out, assuming she did take the thing in the first place...'

Leonard was waiting for the visit; he'd suspected they were looking in the wrong place. The local police turned to him after a JFE (Joint Forces Exercise), the NCA (National Crime Agency) and even CTSFOs (Counter-Terrorist Specialist Firearms Officers) – equipped with ARVs (Armed Response Vehicles) and trained to deal with spree shooters engaged in MTAs (Marauding Terror Attacks) – failed to locate the fugitive. They had rejected his initial offer of assistance with slight disdain, telling him to stay indoors and leave the job to professionals. Eight whole days after the search began – precious time wasted – the DCS (Detective Chief Superintendent) now stood in the doorway of the shack, pleading with him to take charge of the operation. 'I'm asking you as a friend, Leonard. We need you; none of the team at my disposal have your unrivalled tracking ability or intimate knowledge of this coastline.' The chief super paused. 'We behaved badly when you approached us. On behalf of the entire constabulary, I'd like to offer my sincerest apologies for that… there's a dangerous criminal out there. Help us make the public safe again. I've taken the liberty of putting a helicopter on standby for you.' Not one to gloat or make the man beg – he was bigger than that – Leonard accepted the challenge immediately. He would do what he had to; not for his own glory but the good of the community.

'…And make sure you've got some water and Benson's bowl,' Sandra added.

Derek's hunch was that the girl wouldn't be far away; Sarah-Jane had indicated he was the first person she'd met exploring the beach; if this was true, it seemed likely the family would be based nearby. This conviction proved incorrect. Forty minutes later, he'd explored a substantial area in both directions and was running low on enthusiasm and provisions; he shared his thoughts and the last of the water with his (panting) companion. 'I'm afraid we may have to accept the camera's gone.'

'Of course I know what kind of husband I'm going to have. He'll be very bright, left-wing and a historian…' The delicate timbre of Sarah-Jane; it was unmistakable. Mr

Tile spun round and scoured the dunes at the back of the beach in an effort to pinpoint the origin. 'I hope you're not expecting me to eat farmed salmon, Mother...'

He spotted the family group behind the tideline, in a sheltered position at the base of a small mound; she was occupying the centre of a picnic rug, a cuckoo in the nest of two drab dunnocks perched attentively either side of her.

He tried to sound friendly and relaxed. 'Ah, there you are...' He smiled at his audience. 'Sorry to disturb your lunch.'

The male parent, who appeared to have all the substance of a badminton racket, peered at him through thick glasses. 'Can we help you?'

'I'd just like a quick word with Sarah-Jane, if that's alright.'

The mother bird looked at her. 'Do you know this man?'

She stared at Derek impassively. 'No. I saw him on the beach earlier. He's a homeless vagrant. Why do they always have dogs? Don't give him any food; he's on the scrounge. It will only encourage him. And he smells.'

His body underwent a violent spasm. 'If you don't know me, how do I know your name?'

'You asked me, so I told you. I didn't want to appear rude.' She turned to her father. 'He must have followed me here. I'm sorry, Daddy.'

'It's not your fault, my treasure. You've done nothing wrong.' He squinted at Derek. 'I don't think my daughter has anything to say to you. We're having lunch. Perhaps you'd leave us in peace.'

'*Not without my stolen camera!*' There was stunned silence for a few moments. Remembering his wife's advice, Mr Tile struck a more conciliatory note. 'What I mean is, I was showing Sarah-Jane my camera earlier, quite an expensive model actually, and I was wondering if perhaps she'd taken it without noticing. By complete accident, obviously.'

Mrs Dunnock took her daughter's hand. There was a worried expression on her face. 'Do you know anything about a camera, darling?'

She nodded slowly. 'Yes, that's right. The tramp did ask me about a camera. It was a bit odd. "Have you seen my camera?", that's what he said. I told him I hadn't. And then, like he was speaking to someone else, he said, "Sarah-Jane hasn't seen your camera, why don't you show her?" But there wasn't anybody there.'

Mum and Dad glanced at each other in alarm. Mr Dunnock took a phone out of his pocket and cleared his throat. 'I'm asking you politely to go away now. If you don't, I'll call the police.' They all looked at Derek. The girl stuck her tongue out.

Then he remembered something. 'The notebook!' A smile spread across his lips; the smirk disappeared from hers. 'I can prove she's lying. There's a notebook in her bag. She made an entry recording our meeting. I think it begins with "So far I've met a pensioner…" and contains an unflattering appraisal of my sand sculpture.'

Sarah-Jane jumped up. 'I know what's happened!' She pointed a finger at the guilty party. 'You put the camera in my bag.'

'Why would I do that?'

'Because you stole it!' She turned to her parents. 'You heard him, he called it "my stolen camera". I knew I felt something when my back was turned on the beach. You stored it for safekeeping, making me an accomplice. Now you've come to collect it.' She reached behind her. 'I bet we find it in here...' She produced the camera from her bag with an air of triumphant vindication. 'Look, here it is! Just as I thought.'

'I'm calling the police right now,' the father announced. 'As soon as I get a signal.'

'No, Bernard. Unless you want them to arrest our daughter.'

'But, Mummy, a rough sleeper couldn't afford a camera like—'

'*Stop it!*' The woman seemed close to tears. 'Just stop lying, Sarah-Jane.'

'I don't understand,' Bernard chirruped. 'Why don't you believe her story, Barbara?'

'Why?! For god's sake, what's wrong with you? Why? Because she's been expelled from two schools for stealing and lying. Because we're lucky she hasn't been sent away.' Barbara shook her head sadly. 'What you should be doing is pleading with this gentleman not to call the police himself.'

'His name's Derrick. Like the crane.'

*

Mr Tile's young friend would go on to study at Oxford, but not for long. In her second term, she'd be sent down after a number of valuable items belonging to other students were discovered in her room. Put there by someone else, she maintained. Sarah-Jane currently works in private equity. Barbara and Bernard are divorced.

SEVEN

On his return to camp with the camera and one parental apology, Derek elected to seek invigoration and rejuvenated wellbeing through maritime exertion, to go for a dip. Calculating that it was more than an hour since lunch, and therefore the CAP (Cramp Awareness Protocol) no longer applied, he determined the time had come to enter the sea for his daily HAT (Holiday Aquatic Training). This constituted alternate repetitions of the two preferred styles – front crawl and breaststroke – with floating breaks between. In his experience, backstroke was impractical outside a swimming pool setting – ideally a lake-sized, learner-restricted, lane-based, leisure centre one – while his attempts at butterfly, he was reliably informed (by Sandra), bore little resemblance to the fluttering flight of that delicate creature and rather more to the blundering coitus of a novice male walrus.

The exercise programme had been completed with the required commitment and a certain undeniable panache –

several other bathers had stopped what they were doing to admire his technique, staring and shaking their heads as he churned past – allowing Mr Tile to enjoy his reward: a well-earned period of relaxation in the water after the session, lying spreadeagled on his back. He closed his eyes and breathed deeply, letting his mind and body drift, unanchored from anxiety for a few minutes at least.

In Derek's opinion, galeophobia was perfectly natural, healthy even, the sign of a normally functioning survival instinct; what he considered to be abnormal and unnatural was a fish that ate people. Clearly an evolutionary error, no amount of specious reasoning from marine biologists – people who wore a wetsuit to work – would convince him otherwise. So, when he felt something bulky brush against his leg, the reasonable assumption, in the shallows off the Welsh coast, was that he'd come to the attention of a large, hungry shark which had begun to circle him; faced with this mortal danger, the reflexive reaction was to kick out against the predatory threat as hard as he could.

If a motorist crashes into a parked car or other stationary object, it is inevitable the driver's vehicle will suffer some damage and possibly come off worse. Where does the fault lie in this situation? Not a difficult question to answer. As the (almost) stationary object, no responsibility whatsoever could be attached to Mr Tile for the result of the collision. Any damage would be regarded by an insurance company as self-inflicted. The snorkeler hadn't been looking where he was going, too busy staring down below to notice what was straight in front and therefore had to accept the blame for his own injury. It was unfortunate that his forehead had made contact with Derek's foot during the accident with such force, and a degree of bruising did appear likely, but that in no way detracted from the man's legal and moral status as the guilty party. He was the moving object. All this seemed fairly clear-cut and Derek interpreted the silence that followed his nuanced analysis as acceptance of the fact. The snorkeler turned and swam away without audible reply.

Back on shore, there was no practical way, other than being wheeled in a bathing machine, to avoid the distressing consequence of walking across the beach with wet feet – picking up an unpleasant STD (Sandy Toe Disorder). Anticipating this insidious condition, Mr Tile had come fully prepared. Equipment required:

- Bottle of water (large)
- Camping stool
- Foot towel (small)
- Washing-up bowl
- Bath mat
- Garibaldis

After drying himself, the instruments for the procedure needed to be carefully arranged in spatial proximity; he started by positioning the stool in the middle of the carriageway just beyond the M4 junction.

'No. Not there.'

There was a peremptory tone to Sandra's voice which grated, particularly as he'd achieved significantly more (design and construction of M25 sculpture, retrieval of stolen camera against all odds, vigorous aquatic exercise) than she had (occasional alteration of body position) so far that day. This emboldened him. 'Why not?'

'Because we don't want your neurosis on public display.'

There were so many things wrong with this statement it was hard to know where to begin. With the most egregious. 'Having a preference for sand-free toes is not irrational or obsessive.'

'In bed it isn't. On a beach, it is.'

If he couldn't win the argument with her, he would win it without her. By himself, in private. This in no way diminished the victory. He would be fair, conceding that she had made some valid points, before triturating her premise, reasoning and conclusion. The critique would be brilliant and unanswerable, the capitulation complete. She would acknowledge it was ignorant, unacceptable and factually incorrect to accuse him of neurosis; her remorse would be genuine. His wife was smiling at this moment – she clearly had no inkling of the devastating defeat awaiting her.

Derek surveyed the coast knowledgeably, as if gauging something important. 'The breeze is a bit strong out here. It's coming straight off the sea.'

Sandra watched a sailing boat becalmed in the bay. She was diplomatic. 'I agree.'

'I think I'll move back there.' He retired to a more sheltered space between the tent and windbreak to treat his STD.

The camping stool was set up with the washing-up bowl and bath mat laid out symmetrically in front. He placed the foot towel in readiness on the mat, the bottle of water next to the bowl and himself on the stool with the biscuits by his side. The remedy could commence. Dispensing one-third of the water into the bowl, he immersed and washed both feet, concentrating on the toes; the left foot was lifted above the bowl and another third of the bottle poured over it; the clean foot was set down on the mat and dried with the towel; the process was repeated for the right foot; with both feet and all toes now dry and devoid of gritty sand, he replaced his all-terrain sandals (to prevent recurrence) and reached for the garibaldis. Moments later, by complete chance, Benson appeared. Derek shared another biscuit with him, unrolled his second beach towel (for lying, not drying) next to Sandra's, making sure the matching stripes were aligned, and assumed a dual sunbathing/reading position on his front.

He opened Levering's *History* at one of his favourite cases, unusual in the book because no charges were ever brought, and its inclusion relied solely on the testimony of a housekeeper, one Anne Madison. The chapter concerned the death of Nicholas Brann, a business magnate and owner of the London & Berkshire Railway Company, who lived in a grand mansion near the market town of Wokingham. In July 1850 Mr Brann witnessed an event in London which would change his life, ultimately bringing it to a premature end. He was a spectator at Vauxhall Gardens when Charles Green lifted off in a hydrogen-filled balloon with a small pony accompanying him in the basket. Nicholas was astounded by this feat, and from that day devoted himself to the pursuit of a dream: flying his own balloon over the house and lands of the Brann estate; in doing so, he would become the first man in England to survey his property from the air.

Not long after, in January 1851, a young gentleman named George Horner was contracted to the household as a tutor on the instructions of Emma Brann, his wife. Local gossip quickly spread about the nature of Mr Horner's employment, in particular whether he'd gained the position "as much by his degree of looks as learning", and there seems little doubt, according to a number of reports, that certain afternoon activities included on George's timetable were not obviously for the benefit of the children.

Over the next couple of years Nicholas Brann poured his considerable tenacity and resources into the research, development and testing of various prototypes, an obsession in which, unusually perhaps, he was very much encouraged by his wife. George also proved supportive, engaging Nicholas in lengthy discussions about the technical aspects of ballooning – "being most solicitous in his enquiries", in the words of the housekeeper – and suggesting a regular stream of aeronautical lectures and events in London, some lasting several days, which he considered to be of potential interest.

It was at one of these, in August 1852, that Mr Brann saw Madame Poitevin take off from Chelsea's Cremorne Gardens riding on the back of a bull, in a depiction of the Greek goddess Europa. This infamous stunt led to a public outcry after the traumatised bull had to be destroyed, charges of animal cruelty and a change in the law regarding "airborne beasts". A diplomatic incident ensued, with the French ambassador claiming Madame Poitevin's real crime was being a female foreigner who had surpassed the Englishman Charles Green. Nicholas himself regarded it as a remarkable achievement, becoming even more determined to realise his personal ambition within a year.

Finally, in the spring of 1853, the balloon was ready. A date of 16 April was set for the flight, invitations sent out, arrangements made, entertainments planned, the newspapers informed and the location prepared. On the afternoon of the 15th, a small party comprising Brann, his engineer, technician and two assistants assembled at the launch site; also present as onlookers were Emma and George. A tethered flight had been decided on as a rehearsal, allowing for last-minute checks and adjustments to be completed before the big day. All went according to plan: the team readied the balloon, Nicholas climbed aboard and the wicker basket rose in the air; everyone applauded, waiting for the ascent to be arrested by the four mooring ropes. At a height of exactly thirty feet, it reached the limit of the tethers and was held in position, floating above the spectators like a Brobdingnagian toy. Briefly. There followed what one witness described as a loud clanking noise and the metal plate underneath the basket – to which the ropes attached – simply fell away. Now unrestrained and much lighter, the balloon continued rising with increasing speed.

Before aeronautical advances later in the century, the weight of this iron plate served two critical functions: to stabilise the basket during flight and to prevent a dangerous height being attained where air pressure and wind velocity accelerated dramatically; without it, Brann had little chance. Neither the balloon nor his body were recovered.

At this point, Mr Levering expressed the hope that Nicholas gained some satisfaction from fulfilling his dream; Mr Tile suspected he'd be too busy screaming in terror.

Although sabotage was strongly suspected, not least by Anne Madison ("so far from doubts as to be certain"), no proof or supporting evidence existed. A year after the incident, on 15 April 1854, the coroner officially recorded the death of Nicholas Brann as misadventure. The tutor remained in his position – it was thought to be in the best interests of the children to provide continuity – while the housekeeper did not. The marriage of George Horner and Emma Brann (widowed) is listed in the Church archives for Wokingham parish as taking place in January 1855, four years after fate placed them together.

As a footnote, Cornelius Levering revealed that while George's father was a legal clerk by profession, his maternal grandfather, who lived with the family in old age, had been a blacksmith.

Derek closed the *History of Noteworthy Felonies* and then his eyes. He slept immediately, dreaming that he was trapped inside Brann's balloon, lying on his towel but falling, material flapping against his face as the envelope decompressed. Sandra lifted a fold from his head. 'It's four o'clock. Time to go.' She had collapsed the tent and was packing up, anticipating a glass of chilled wine on their return. Like a camel, Derek got to his feet in a series of reluctant rocking movements; he was not looking forward to humping everything back across the sand.

As they entered the caravan meadow, one ambling the other lurching, Lee drove past them at high speed with the windows down and music up. 'Terek!' The SUV skidded to a halt.

Mrs Tile looked at her husband. 'Does he mean you?'

'I think he does. That's our neighbour.'

She put her hand on his arm. 'Remember, when we left for the beach, the dog was fine. As far as you know, it still is… I'll go on.'

The driver turned the engine off and got out of the car. Derek turned to face him cheerfully. 'Greetings. Been a lovely day.'

'Not if you're JJ.' Lee pointed at the boot. 'He's in there.'

'Shouldn't you let him out?'

'What for, a walk? Stretch of legs? You're right, he must be getting a bit stiff by now... JJ's dead. The vet came two hours ago.'

'Really? What happened?'

'Not sure yet. I found him lying on the ground.' He took a couple of deep breaths. 'That's why I wanted a word, Terek.' Lee leant forward conspiratorially. 'Did you notice anyone hanging around this morning?'

'Nobody who alerted suspicion. A jogger. Other people staying here. Why?'

'JJ didn't have a scratch on him. But there were these bits of chicken in his teeth. He's not had that from us, so where did it come from? Kay reckons he got it underneath the van.'

'Sounds plausible. Is the chicken important?'

'Maybe, maybe not. Did the chicken kill the dog? Depends on the post-mortem.'

Derek steered the conversation in a different direction. 'Where are you taking him?'

'Heaven. Otherwise known as Staines. I want it done by people I know... then get him cremated. JJ loved swimming in the sea, so that's where I'm scattering the ashes.' He steered it back again. 'Of course, there's always a chance that chicken could be something else.'

'Like turkey?'

'Deliberate. Poisoned meat. Given to JJ for a reason.'

'Why would someone do that?'

'To get back at me. Because they had a grudge.' Lee cracked his knuckles. 'And I reckon I know who that person could be, Tezza.'

'Do you?'

Lee nodded. 'The chef at breakfast.'

'Kay?'

'No. We went to the restaurant. Had a bit of a run-in with the bloke at the omelette station. I took mine back, it was like chewing a carpet sample. I told him: "I'm after something to eat, not put down in the living room. Make me another one, the dog can have this." He didn't like that much. Asked what table we were at. Which is how he found out where we were staying, I reckon. Easy enough for him to get hold of the chicken and put something in it.'

'What are you going to do?'

'Depends what the vet says. If that chef hurt JJ, then I'll hurt him. Warm his bollocks with a blow torch. Either way, I won't be having another omelette. See you Saturday. I'm coming back then.'

Lee got back in the car and sped off; Derek didn't move for quite a long time. This development provided serious cause for concern: it appeared the process had been interrupted, the circulation had become obstructed; without warning, the cycle of cause and effect seemed to have shifted out of alignment. The evidence suggested a UDE (Unknown Disruptive Event) had occurred. If the mechanism was impaired then remedial action needed to be taken; something had to be done – Sandra would know what – as soon as possible. He found her sitting outside the static home with a chilled glass of wine. 'How did it go?' she asked him.

'We've got a problem, my love.'

'Is it serious?'

'The flow of the system has malfunctioned.' He explained the complication that had arisen regarding the omelette chef.

She looked at him. 'I think it might be time for some KIP, Mr Tile.'

He met her gaze. 'It could well be, Mrs Tile.'

Preparation was required before they could begin – a conducive atmosphere and setting needed to be created. The curtains and living room door were closed; the middle of the floor was cleared and the coffee table placed at the front; rugs and cushions were arranged to ensure comfort; a laptop was set up on the table. While Sandra lit some scented candles she'd brought for this eventuality, Derek turned off the lights and accessed the internet. They undressed and sat cross-legged with their backs straight, hands resting on knees and eyes closed, performing the introductory breathing exercises for several minutes. When they were settled, Mr Tile leant forward and clicked on the YouTube video; KIP (Karma Integrated Plumbing) commenced. The screen showed a chubby, middle-aged man standing in a loft next to a water tank. He had receding hair, wore a pink polo shirt, and a gold chain was visible round his neck. '*Welcome to the tutorial; my name's Terry... so, we've traced the water coming into the property via the rising main, feeding the downstairs appliances at the same plumbing pressure as the supply.*'

'Plumbing pressure,' the Tiles chanted in unison. Quietly, Sandra hummed a few bars of the 1981 chart-topper "Under Pressure".

On screen, Terry lifted the lid of the tank. '*When the water comes into the property, it branches off to feed the downstairs appliances, and one branch of it comes upstairs directly into the cold-water tank.*' Terry stopped for a minute to collect his thoughts. He glanced surreptitiously at the palm of his hand. '*Now, the level of the cold-water tank is set by a float valve.*' The screen showed the inside of the tank. There was the sound of running water. '*And you can see that when I push this float valve down, the water comes in. As the water rises…*'

'Water rises,' they chanted.

'*…it lifts the float, and that automatically shuts off the supply to the tank.*' The screen showed Terry holding the lid again. '*As soon as you open a tap upstairs, and the cold water is allowed to flow out…*'

'Water flows out.'

'*…this allows the float to drop, which allows the main's water to come back into the tank, so it keeps the tank at a constant level.*'

'Keeps a constant level.'

'*The white tube that you can see at the end of the tank is the overflow.*' The screen showed Terry's fingers next to the pipe. It looked like a straw in comparison. '*So, if this float valve doesn't shut off the cold-water supply, and the water rises higher than it should do, the surplus water will go out through the overflow.*'

'Surplus through the overflow.'

The screen returned to Terry in the loft. He was adjusting his own pipework. '*That travels down through the network, through the property, through the outside wall and there will be a visible sign…*'

'There will be a visible sign.'

'...that your tank is overflowing. And that visible sign is the overflow sticking out of the wall, and you can watch the water running out of it, if your tank is overflowing.' At this point, Terry got distracted and seemed to momentarily lose his way. He looked around as if wondering what he was doing in a loft talking to a water tank. 'So, that's where the water comes from the rising main, up into the cold-water tank. It connects everything in your system.'

'It connects everything in the system.'

'Everything in the system connects.'

The screen showed pipes going down through the floor of the loft. 'This tank is set above, obviously, in the loft space.' The screen showed Terry in the loft space again. He hastily returned a half-eaten Twix to his pocket. 'It's set above those taps and the distance between this tank and the taps that it feeds at the lower level is called the head. So, the higher that tank is in the air, the greater the head, the greater the pressure of water feeding the upstairs taps.'

'The higher, the greater.'

'The greater, the higher.'

'Again, to recap, water comes into the property through the rising main. Part of that feeds the downstairs and the other part of it comes up to the cold-water tank.' The screen showed pipes coming up through the floor and into the tank. 'You can see if it's overflowing, so you know if there's something wrong.' The screen showed a close-up of Terry's neck and head. He was sweating. The gold chain had the letter T on the end. 'So, that's where the water goes, how it flows, when it's come into the property.'

'Where it goes is how it flows,

'Where it flows is how it goes.

'How it flows is where it goes,

'How it goes is where it flows!'

Confident the system was now fully restored to working order, Derek turned the video off.

Outside, a figure stood on the path by the side of the meadow, watching the caravan. The woman was in her late forties, wearing jogging kit, with her long, black hair tied in a ponytail. She hesitated; the lights were off and the curtains closed; it didn't look like anyone was there. A decision was made – she carried on running.

EIGHT

Having slept well and woken early on Friday morning, the Tiles embarked on a pre-breakfast beach walk with a purpose. They made a right turn below the hotel and headed in the opposite direction to the day before, towards the jetty where the hire boats were moored. This facility had been shut since their arrival but, according to the DIB (Daily Intelligence Briefing) from Sandra's new friend Gwyn on reception, it opened at the weekends in June. Encouragingly, there were signs of life as they approached – the cover had been removed from one of the outboards and somebody was busy working on the engine. 'Greetings!' Derek called.

The man looked round. 'Closed today, we are.'

'Yes. We're interested in the possibility of booking something today for our employment—'

'No can do.' The boatman resumed his repairs.

'...when we come back tomorrow.'

'Come back tomorrow, that's right.'

'I don't think he understood you,' Sandra observed.

'I'm aware of the current misunderstanding, thank you.' Derek waved. 'Hello... excuse me!'

The man shook his head. 'What now?'

'We don't want a boat today.'

'That's good. Because you can't have one.'

'We'd like it tomorrow.'

'It's not about like. There's no choice in the matter. Closed today, open tomorrow.'

As the boatman turned his back, Mrs Tile made an executive decision. 'Not going very well, is it? I think I'd better talk to him.'

She returned five minutes later having reserved one of the motorboats (with steering wheel, as stipulated) for Saturday morning. Derek spied an opportunity to regain some lost territory. 'The afternoon would be better. It's quieter.' He walked onto the jetty. 'Hello...'

The man looked up. 'Here we go again.'

'Is it possible to change the morning to the afternoon?'

'Not without a time machine, and we don't rent them. Most people want boats.'

'Yes.' Derek tried asking the same question in a different form. 'Can I alter the booking my wife just made to later in the day?'

'No, you can't.'

'Why not?'

'You didn't make the booking.'

There was silence for a moment. Mr Tile twitched. He cleared his throat. 'Imagine this scenario: we've gone for breakfast together. I need to make a phone call in private, so I ask you to order for me.'

'If you like. What is it you're having?'

'The food selection has no relevance to the point I'm trying to make.'

'I think it does.' The boatman sat back and folded his arms. 'I can't order for you if you don't tell me what you want.'

'Cereal and toast.'

'That's two breakfasts.'

'No, it isn't.'

'Two dishes. Two breakfasts. I'm not ordering twice for you.'

Derek could see that Sandra was about to run out of patience. 'Fine. I'll have the same as you… now, I leave the table to make a call. The waiter comes and you order for both of us. I return to the table… right, what did you get me?'

'Nothing.'

'What do you mean?'

'I've had breakfast.'

Derek's body spasmed violently. 'Let's be clear. Have you ordered anything at all?'

'No. You wanted the same as me. Which was nothing.'

Sandra had run out of patience. She walked onto the jetty. 'Sorry to interrupt.' She looked at her husband. 'Any chance I could have some breakfast today?'

The man looked at Sandra. 'Am I ordering your breakfast as well?'

'Excuse me?'

Derek saw his opening. 'Glad you're here, my love. Just sorting out this booking. We'd like to change it to the afternoon, wouldn't we?'

'If that's what you want, then yes.'

He turned to the boatman. 'You hear that? The preferred time slot has now moved from Saturday morning to Saturday afternoon. It's possible to accommodate this temporal adjustment in your reservation platform, is it?'

'No problem.'

He turned to Sandra confidently. 'Would you mind adjudicating on something for us? In your opinion, does cereal and toast count as one breakfast or two?'

She considered for a moment. 'Two. It can't be served on one dish.'

This was obviously incorrect, Derek reflected as they walked back along the beach to the hotel restaurant, rueing the rash and unnecessary arbitration request he'd made to his wife. In group discussions where an erroneous consensus had been reached, there were generally two options: spend considerable time and effort explaining to other participants the fallacious basis of their opinions, often resulting in general embarrassment and, unfortunately, a certain degree of bad feeling, or submit recent events to the process of RCE (Retrospective Conversation Editing). This technique had a number of distinct advantages:

- It didn't involve anyone else.
- There was no need for irrelevant debate.
- The outcome would not be questioned.
- Everybody was happy.

Simpler, quicker and less controversial than compromise-based models, RCE represented a major advancement in the field of conflict resolution, with potential applications across a broad spectrum of arenas; in this instance it bridged categories, touching on the culinary, nautical and interpersonal. Mr Tile felt that a few minor tweaks would produce a more authentic version of the jetty episode:

DEREK: Would you mind adjudicating on something for us? In your opinion, does cereal and toast count as one breakfast or two?

SANDRA: One. Unquestionably. In fact, I'm surprised anyone would even suggest that cereal and toast could be considered two breakfasts.

Pause

BOATMAN: *(To SANDRA)* I admit that was me, to my shame. *(To DEREK).* Sorry, you were right all along. I was wrong, so very wrong! It's complete rubbish, I see that now. Wrong about the breakfast and the booking. I tried to be clever, but it backfired. By way of apology, would you take the boat for your entire stay? Be my guest; it's the least I can do. No charge at all.

DEREK: That won't be necessary; we've all got to make a living. See you tomorrow.

SANDRA: I'm very proud of you, Derek Tile.

He took her hand as they watched the tide coming in over the sand, observing how the line of water edged forward unevenly, sporadically, the vanguard continually shifting, like a herd of grazing cattle moving across a field. The Tiles climbed the steps to the restaurant terrace. Everybody was happy.

A single boiled egg with one piece of toast – unquestionably a quarter breakfast, in Derek's view – was all the Dietary Commission permitted, calorie intake being strictly regulated in anticipation of a big lunch. While he went on an information-gathering journey to the omelette station, his wife texted her sister to find out what time they were expected. In the middle of this composition, Sandra became aware that a man had stopped in front of their table. 'You're one of us, aren't you?' he volunteered. She ignored this opening gambit in the hope he'd move on and try it somewhere else. He didn't. 'I know one when I see one. You're a Meadower.'

She looked up. He was wearing a blue cap emblazoned with the word "ROTARY" and a large wheel in gold. 'Sorry, I'm just sending a message.' Assuming this would be clear enough, she carried on.

'Staying in one of the caravans. A member of the club, like us. We're in Number Five on this occasion... we saw you yesterday afternoon, walking back down the meadow. Been to the beach, we thought. My name's Bill.'

She gave up. 'Sandra.'

'Your first visit?'

'Staying here it is, yes.'

'Takes a bit of getting used to, that's what we've found. Of course, it's changed over time. Fifteen years ago, the place was very different.' Bill eyed the spare chair. 'There's some interesting stories, if you're not in a rush…'

'We're about to leave, actually.' She made a show of gathering her things. 'Need to get ready, we're going out for the day. Nice to meet you.'

'Hear about that dog?'

'I did.'

'Everyone's talking about it. Nasty business… up your end, wasn't it?'

'I believe so.'

'All kinds of theories going round. I've got one of my own.' He checked in both directions, then leant over the table. 'Gypsies.'

'Right. Any particular reason, apart from the obvious?'

Bill seemed delighted with the question, grinning and nodding his approval as if she'd just invited him to a swingers' quiz night. 'I had a feeling we'd get on. She looks like our kind of person, that's what I told the wife… it is obvious, isn't it? They couldn't resist the caravans. Drawn to them, gypsies are. Not allowed to say that though. Verboten, in the current climate. The way things are going, there's bound to be a law against it soon… what I think happened was a gang of pikeys came down on a thieving expedition and got attacked by the dog. They returned later and poisoned it. I'd put money on that if—'

Derek approached the table. 'Ready to go, my love?'

Bill peered at the new arrival. 'It's you, it really is…' The stare became a glare. 'The sea thug! The marine mugger!'

'Have we met?'

'Oh, yes. We've met all right.' He tore off his cap. Underneath the wheel, a mottled disc of bruising surrounded a dark, swollen hub. About the size of a heel. 'My forehead is on intimate terms with your foot. Look! You did this. It's assault.'

Sandra seemed quite impressed. 'Did you, really?'

'Self-defence,' Derek assured her. 'He swam into me. An instinctive reaction. No blame can be apportioned to someone floating on their back.'

'I brushed against you!' Bill insisted. 'Next thing I know, this lout launches a full-scale aqua attack. Kicking out hard like I was a shark. See this?' He pointed to the angry contusion discolouring his forehead. 'That is not self-defence. I bet there's not a mark on you. One minute I'm snorkelling quite happily—'

'Snorkelling?' Mrs Tile checked. 'Not in the designated swimming area, I hope?'

'Where's that?'

'Between the yellow and black flags. You've heard of the WASP law?' Bill shook his head. 'Women Against Snorkelling Pests. The Welsh parliament passed legislation this year to prevent men in masks harassing female swimmers. They get stung with a fine then a beach ban.'

'I had no idea,' Bill protested. 'I wasn't being a pest.'

'Clearly distracted by something in the water, though,' Derek pointed out. 'Not an abundance of tropical fish and coral reefs in the Bristol Channel.'

'If it happens again, I'll have to notify the authorities,' she warned. 'But there's no need to take the matter any further for now. We are neighbours, after all.'

'Thank you, Sandra… ignorance is no excuse. My conduct was unbefitting the treasurer of Christchurch Rotarians. I will consider this a wake-up call and serve a two-week suspension with immediate effect.' Bill replaced his cap and left.

In no rush, she sipped her lemon and ginger tea. It tasted sweet. 'How did it go?'

'Confirmed omelette-station altercation yesterday,' Mr Tile reported, 'between an aggressive guest and one of the chefs.'

'That sounds like Lee. And he's made a direct connection with the dog.' During the ensuing pause, she smiled. 'Which should prove a minor glitch now the system's reset.' Sandra's phone pinged with an incoming text; as she read, the good humour ebbed through furrows in her brow. 'It's from Yvette. Another change of plan... we're now being offered a picnic lunch at half-one. She's taking Ken to see the physio. His back's playing up again.'

'What a shame, poor old Kenneth,' Derek said. Derek thought: *SAT (Shortened Afternoon Torture) thanks to NAV (Non-Active Valetudinarian)*.

The Tiles agreed that combining a slightly earlier departure with the later arrival would create the opportunity for a diversion on the way to Yvette and Ken's; reaching a consensus on the destination was more difficult.

'Let's put it to a vote,' Derek suggested.

'If you like. Llangarloc is my choice.

'I cast my ballot for Kidwelly.'

'It's a tie,' the returning officer announced to a crowded sports hall. 'And since I get the casting vote,' she continued, 'Llangarloc wins.'

'Why do you get the casting vote?'

'An equal, democratic relationship between mature adults is like riding a tandem. We're both pedalling; we're both contributing… it's just that I'm contributing slightly more.'

'How?'

'I'm steering.'

Amended itinerary for outbound leg:

- Original departure time: 10:55.
- Original arrival time: 12:25.
- Revised departure time: 10:25.
- Revised arrival time: 13:25.
- Original journey duration: one hour and thirty minutes.
- Revised journey duration: Approx. three hours.
- Route: B-roads to A4118; A4118, A4216, A4883 to M4 J47; J47 to J49; at J49 take A48 to Carmarthen; A40 to Haverfordwest; B-roads to house. New diversion off A40; A478 to Llangarloc.
- Time travelling to and from diversion destination: thirty minutes.
- Time at diversion destination: Approx. one hour.
- Reason for victory of diversion destination: "a buzzy little place full of boutiques and lovely independent shops" (Gwyn). Strong pitch with clear message targeting highly motivated constituency.
- Sandra's expectation of Llangarloc expressed in plant form: sunflower.
- Derek's expectation of Llangarloc expressed in plant form: death cap.[1]

---

1 Entry disallowed. "Mushrooms are fungi" (Sandra).

- Rival destination for diversion: Kidwelly Industrial Museum (KIM).
- Reasons for defeat of rival destination: museum's focus on tinplate industry, coal mining and brickmaking failed to attract key voter demographic. KIM's absence of buzz, boutiques and lovely independent shops during campaign amounted to electoral suicide in retail heartlands.
- Subject of second ballot prior to departure: proposal for electoral reform entailing abolition of casting vote.
- Number in favour of electoral reform: One.
- Number against electoral reform: One.
- Result of ballot after application of casting vote: proposal defeated.
- Prospect of electoral reform: remote.
- Mood of Llangarloc supporters during journey: delectation.
- Mood of Kidwelly supporters during journey: resignation.

After fifteen minutes, Mr Tiles' suspicions about the town had been confirmed – it contained absolutely nothing of any interest, resembling a large open prison with shops, not dramatically unpleasant but so mundanely depressing that being confined there – where life definitely wasn't – constituted punishment enough. He decided to return to the park with Benson and practise retirement by sitting alone on a bench in the middle of a weekday, discussing existence with the ducks.

Derek retraced his steps, taking a reckless shortcut down a side street where he passed a sign for The Llangarloc Archive; reasoning that doing something was better than nothing (and if not, he could take it up with the ducks afterwards), he went inside. Entry was free – voluntary donations at the end welcome – the curator friendly and dogs allowed. The archive consisted of one large room, divided into sections; the first was labelled "Non-Motorised Land Transport". The exhibits on show were a skateboard, trike, toboggan, pushchair, hand cart, pedal car, snowboard, kite buggy, three bicycles, skis, pogo stick, wheelchair, roller skates, ice skates, child's scooter, sledge and space hopper. Any connection to the town was unclear.

The next display was titled "Natural World", with five objects available for inspection: a tree branch (elm) carried from Swansea in the 1977 hurricane; a semi-melted wheelie bin (green) struck by lightning in 2001; a blackened rock that formed part of an asteroid deposited on a supermarket (Tesco) in 1962; a road sign (30) with a water mark from the 2014 floods; and a section of car roof (Fiat) dented by freak hailstones in 1989.

"Celebrity" held thirteen items:

1. Monogrammed cushion from Tom Jones's stairlift.
2. Striped swimming trunks owned by David Lloyd George.
3. Jigsaw of Hollywood Hills that belonged to the young Catherine Zeta-Jones.
4. Wallet, house keys, cigarettes and condom left in a pub by Dylan Thomas.
5. Nye Bevan's jodhpurs and riding crop.
6. Dartboard and oche marker owned by Shirley Bassey.
7. Travel compact with magnifying mirror carried by Richard Burton.

8. Welsh Collie (stuffed) which died after being touched by Margaret Thatcher.
9. Manchester United F.C. (away strip) pyjamas worn by Ryan Giggs.
10. Photo of Prince Edward performing as Cinderella in Tenby's pantomime.
11. Bottle of Michael Heseltine's bespoke hair dye from a salon in Swansea.
12. Carmarthenshire Junior Tennis Cup won by John Cale.
13. Gold medallion left in a hotel room by Neil Kinnock.

Beginning to suspect that the town archive was a con similar in scale to The Home of the Oranmore Hermit in County Galway (five euros bought a four-mile, uphill trek to a cave with a three-legged stool), Mr Tile approached "Infamy" without much hope. His initial impression wasn't promising: an unexceptional, antique armchair occupied the middle of a narrow cubicle; it needed completely reupholstering and bore evidence of historic fire damage. A small plaque explained why:

> *This chair was the sole item saved from the home of Eliza Bowen – The Harlot of Llangarloc – after a mob burned her cottage to the ground in December 1906.*

That was it; the cubicle contained nothing else. However, this snippet of information piqued his curiosity and Derek sought out the curator. He found her behind the desk at the entrance, working on the computer.

She finished typing, sat back and smiled. 'Eliza Bowen, now that is a story.'

'Yes, I'd like to know more. Do you have any leaflets?'

'We don't, I'm afraid... I probably know as much as anyone though.'

He saw her eyes dart in the direction of the donation box. He looked in his wallet – there were three ten-pound notes, nothing smaller. After some hesitation, a tenner was generously contributed to the running costs of the archive. 'Did she survive the fire?'

'She wasn't there. Eliza had been warned. We don't know by whom, but she fled with her daughter to Cardiff. She had family in the city.'

'What had she done?'

'Primarily, rejected the advances of the Reverend Thomas Durd, minister of Llangarloc Presbyterian Church. He offered to support her on a quid pro quo basis; she flatly refused... Eliza's second offence was the sin of supplying her homemade cosmetics to most women in the area, some of them presumably members of the very congregation incited by Thomas Durd... bear in mind that make-up was frowned upon in 1906, not sold openly or widely available outside the big cities. It was still associated with prostitution and the stage, so Eliza's clandestine business provided an easy target from the pulpit.'

'And the fact she wasn't married?'

'She was, actually. But her husband walked out when the child was two. Faced with the workhouse or the conditional charity of the Good Reverend, Eliza had to find a way to make ends meet. And quick. Already expert at making beauty products for herself, she expanded production and established her own cottage industry, literally, under the thatch.' The curator broke off at this point and looked at the time. 'I'd better get on with some work; the quarterly rent's due at the end of the month.'

Mr Tile reached for his wallet again. 'Twenty pounds to hear the rest of the story.'

'Done... right, records show that Eliza Bowen and her daughter lived in Cardiff until 1908, when they emigrated to America. In New York she became an agent for the California Perfume Company, later called Avon, and married an executive named David Scheele in 1911. They had two children of their own and the family of five moved to Westchester County in 1916. Which is all we know about Eliza... however, that same year, Reverend Durd was also on the move, in a prison van to Cardiff Gaol. He was reported for preaching anti-war sermons by members of his congregation who had lost loved ones in the conflict. Convicted of sedition under the Defence of the Realm Act, he got a sentence of five years. Prison was not a happy experience for Thomas. The clergyman wrote desperate letters to the diocese, stating that he was being assaulted on a daily basis. The term he used was catamite. In response, the Bishop of Swansea defrocked him. There seems to have been a conversion to the communist cause, swapping one orthodoxy for another, and a move to Germany after his release, because the last record we have is a 1926 newspaper account of a street riot in Berlin. Among those killed on the anti-fascist side was a foreigner named Mr Thomas Durd, a card-carrying brigade member from Wales.' The curator finished the story and got up. 'Would you hold on a minute?' She disappeared into a back room and returned holding a camera. 'Can I take your picture?'

Derek was too surprised to question her. 'If you like… here?'

'Next to Eliza's chair, if you don't mind.' She directed him into position and got the shot desired. 'Great. Thank you.'

'This piece was donated, I imagine?'

'It was, by me. It belonged to my mother. I never liked it. And she ruined it anyway by dropping a cigarette down the side. One too many gins. The thing caught fire. It was nearly a disaster.'

Mr Tile caught himself gawping at her. 'The chair has no connection to Eliza Bowen?'

'None at all,' she confirmed. 'But you need a prop to grab the punters' attention. It's part of the theatre.'

He looked round the room. 'Are any of these objects authentic?'

'I'd say about two-thirds. A bit more, maybe. Seventy per cent… does it really matter? Some are genuine, some not. Our lives are a farrago of fact and fiction, about ourselves, about other people. And that's the way we like it. I bet there are some items here you'd be more upset to discover were fakes than others.'

He thought this over. 'What about the road sign?'

The curator laughed. 'Yes, it's a real sign from the 2014 floods. But why did you single it out from everything else? That's a more interesting question… entrance to the archive is free; the only transaction is between visitor and exhibit. It's a dialogue unique to each one of us. We hear our own stories echoed in the world.'

Waiting back at the car, Sandra was pleased to see her husband looked in a good mood as he approached. It boded well for the rest of the afternoon. 'Did you like Llangarloc in the end?'

'I rushed to judgement and jumped to conclusions. I was wrong, my love. It's a palace of serendipity... how about you?'

'I found a couple of nice things, then ran out of time. We've bought Yvette some flowers. Perhaps you'd like to give them to her?'

The in-Jag ambience was relaxed as they drove through the town and out onto the A478, listening to "Genesis" by Genesis on the CD player.

*

Two weeks later, a framed photograph of Derek standing next to Eliza's chair would appear in the cubicle. Beside it was a plaque with the date and a short description:

> *The great-grandson of Eliza Bowen, David Scheele IV*
> *from New York State U.S.A., visits the archive.*
> *The trustees are grateful for his generous donation.*

If the curator happened to be giving a talk about Eliza to a visiting party of tourists, pensioners or schoolchildren, Mr Tile's profession would vary according to her mood. On some occasions, she'd make him a theme park designer, sports agent or radiator manufacturer, on others an entomologist, dressage judge or Broadway producer. Once, for the whole of October, Derek became a farmer.

LUNCH

ACT I

The patio of a house in the country. SANDRA and YVETTE are setting a table. KEN hobbles across the terrace with a stick, assisted by DEREK.

KEN: *(to DEREK)* Not so fast... my back's very tender after the pummelling I've just had.

DEREK: Come along, Kenneth, nearly there.

KEN: *(to DEREK)* Wait, I need a break... the pain's excruciating.

DEREK: *(to KEN)* A few more steps... would you mind not elbowing me?

KEN: Not sure I can make it… you might all have to say goodbye to me right here.

SANDRA: *(to YVETTE, loudly)* This Chablis looks nice. Derek's driving so it could be down to the two of us.

YVETTE: I'm sure we'll manage.

KEN: Let's go, Derek. We've got this… it's not my style to be a wet weekend.

DEREK: You just elbowed me again… *(helps KEN into a chair)* watch out with that stick of yours… there you are.

KEN: Complete torture, I tell you.

YVETTE: Not bad, Derrykins. Maybe you could become a nurse if you ever get bored of road-watching.

DEREK: *(to YVETTE)* What age was it yesterday?

SANDRA: *(to DEREK)* Well done, thank you. What would you like to drink, cold lemonade?

DEREK: *(sits next to KEN)* Just some water will do.

YVETTE:	*(to DEREK)* Not there! You're over here, next to me. Boy, girl, boy, girl... that's it.
KEN:	Pour the wine then, someone... well done, Sandra... leave the bottle there... cheers!
SANDRA:	*(to Yvette)* Happy Birthday!
YVETTE:	Happy Friday! And welcome... I didn't have time to do much so it's just a few bits from the fridge. Please help yourselves.
KEN:	Thank you, Mrs Waitrose.
YVETTE:	I made the chutney.

KEN, SANDRA and DEREK exchange glances. For a few minutes, all four of them are occupied with passing plates, serving food etc.

SANDRA:	*(to DEREK)* Where's Benson? Unlike him not to appear when there's food...
DEREK:	Residing up the garden. I gave him a sausage roll.
YVETTE:	You didn't... they're not for dogs.
DEREK:	I agree... *(to KEN)* Did the physiotherapist question you about exercise?

KEN: She gave me some exercises to do, if
              that's what you mean… rolling round
              on my back, hooking some strap under
              my foot and stretching, standing on one
              leg… as far as advice goes, cut out the
              soft drinks… *(helping himself to more
              wine)* nothing alcohol-free.

YVETTE: *(to SANDRA)* It's a losing battle.

SANDRA: *(to KEN)* Nobody's suggested any
              lifestyle changes?

KEN: I've already made some. I'm practically
              retired these days. Not really
              involved in the day-to-day running
              of the business… avoid stress and
              confrontation, that's the key. You should
              remember that, Sister-In-Law.

SANDRA: *(to KEN)* Give me a top-up then.

KEN: You'll have to steal it. Can't reach over
              there, I'm afraid.

SANDRA: *(to YVETTE)* More for you?

YVETTE: Just a bit.

SANDRA: How are the kids?

YVETTE:	You know, busy with their own lives... Liz still loves New York and her job. She's doing really well at Revlon, seems to enjoy working there. I think she feels appreciated... Tom and her have got an apartment together now.
SANDRA:	Have they? When did that happen?
YVETTE:	Not long ago. A couple of months maybe... she only told me last week. You know what Liz is like – she doesn't give much away.
DEREK:	Yes. What does Thomas do again?
KEN:	He's a communist.
YVETTE:	Tom's a journalist, Derek. Writes for various websites... he's a lovely boy but does come across as slightly evangelical at times...
KEN:	A hypocrite playing at student politics aged thirty, who can only afford to live in Brooklyn and be so morally superior because Elizabeth has a good job and pays the rent. It won't last. She'll get fed up with supporting him... why the Americans haven't locked him up is beyond me.

YVETTE: *(to KEN)* Liz doesn't pay the rent.

KEN: Who does then?

YVETTE: There isn't any. They bought the apartment. Outright.

KEN: What?! How?

YVETTE: Tom paid. And put it in both their names. Liz asked me not to tell you. She wants you to like him for who he is.

Pause

KEN: I do. I've always been very keen on Tom... he's an idealist. I respect that.

DEREK: Where did all the money come from?

YVETTE: Tom's father was in the music business. He set up a record label, sold it for a fortune, then promptly died aged fifty-four.

SANDRA: Sounds like the perfect parent.

YVETTE: That's exactly what Jonny said.

SANDRA: How is Jonny? Still with that beautiful girl?

YVETTE: Rebecca. He is. Pottering around in their funny little cottage making furniture and pheasant casserole. Becca's qualified now, she's a practising equine vet... *(glances at KEN)* we're still hopeful Jonny will go back to law.

KEN: Soon. And stop pissing about.

YVETTE: I worry that carpentry's a hobby in the long-term, not a career.

DEREK: Ole Kirk Christiansen didn't do badly.

YVETTE: Who's he?

DEREK: The Danish carpenter who invented Lego. It was wooden originally... Harrison Ford, Jesus, Ronnie Biggs. All started out as chippies before they hit the big time.

YVETTE: Thank you, Derek. Call me an old-fashioned snob...

SANDRA: Never.

YVETTE: ...But it's unlikely to pay for a nice house, exotic holidays and all the things he grew up with... Jonny might not be thinking about that but I wonder if Becca has. Or will.

SANDRA:	Maybe that's not his goal. He's more of an idealist.
KEN:	Unfortunately for him, his father wasn't a music mogul. And he's not dead.
SANDRA:	Not yet, Ken.
KEN:	The main problem with Jonny's woodwork is, it's crap.
SANDRA:	Worse than yours?
KEN:	Imagine that.
SANDRA:	I'm trying... they could always come and live in your annex I suppose, if they want to save money.
KEN:	No, they can't. Yvette's rented it out.
SANDRA:	Have you?
YVETTE:	Only on a temporary basis, while he's getting divorced.
DEREK:	Who's getting divorced?
KEN:	George.
SANDRA:	That doesn't sound very temporary.

KEN: Tends not to be, I agree.

SANDRA: *(to YVETTE)* Where did George come
                from?

YVETTE: He runs the outdoor activities centre
                in the village. It's a children's charity...
                you can ask him about it yourself.
                He's finishing early today because he's
                working all weekend. I invited him for
                a drink.

SANDRA: How hospitable of you.

KEN: We're not going to have enough cold
                wine, Yvette. There's only one more
                of these in the fridge. I'd put another
                couple of bottles in there while you're
                up.

YVETTE: Yes, sir.

KEN: Well, I can't really do it myself.

YVETTE: *(stands up)* No, so perhaps you should
                slow down a bit.

YVETTE exits across the terrace and into the house.

SANDRA: *(clears plates)* I'll bring a jug of water as
                well.

SANDRA exits the same way as YVETTE. An awkward silence between Derek and Ken for a while.

DEREK: How did you hurt your back then, Kenneth?

KEN: Jury service. It's criminal how uncomfortable the benches are in Swansea Crown Court. I'm considering legal action. The defendant was cleared of all charges, but it was a terrible trial for my back.

DEREK: What was the case?

KEN: A woman, aged forty-three, fought off the Viagra-fuelled sexual advances of an eighty-nine-year-old man by hitting him with a hammer. She was accused of attempted murder.

DEREK: That sounds like self-defence to me. The use of force seems reasonable; the charge certainly doesn't. Were the circumstances suspicious?

KEN: Jackie Laver was cleaning Owen Winter's flat when the incident happened in April last year. He'd arranged to have sex there with a younger woman.

DEREK: He might have struggled to find someone older.

KEN: True. Our pensioner proved nothing if not pragmatic... anyway, when this woman doesn't turn up for the appointment, Owen tells Jackie, and I'm quoting here: "I've already taken my Viagra. You are doing it." Now, it turns out there's history between them. The pair had known each other for several years and Ms Laver admitted she'd previously had sex with Mr Winter, as well as being in the flat when he had sex with other women.

DEREK: Incomprehensible but irrelevant.

KEN: Exactly. Owen himself told the court that he'd asked Jackie to visit him on the day in question as he was expecting a woman called Helen and believed Ms Laver's presence would make her "feel comfortable"... after twenty minutes, verdict from the jury benches: not guilty of attempted murder. After twenty hours, verdict *on* the jury benches: guilty of lumbar assault.

DEREK: Weren't there any cushions available?

KEN: Only these really small ones, like you get in church.

DEREK: Interesting… it could be an arrangement between the synod and judiciary. Soft furnishings in return for legal protection. What colour were they?

KEN: Red. With a nice, embroidered pattern round the border. The design was slightly ecclesiastical, now you mention it.

Pause

DEREK: How are you going to spend your time, if you're retiring?

KEN: Ballooning.

DEREK: In weight?

KEN: Aeronautically… I've caught the bug.

DEREK: When did infection occur?

KEN: Last year. We were at this charity auction in December and one of the lots was a trip for two in a hot-air balloon. Yvette won the bidding, got a bit carried away in fact. I thought we were going over the Pacific, not Pembrokeshire, for that price... we both forgot about it until the company called one afternoon in January and asked if we were free at the weekend... it was awe-inspiring, floating in a lighter-than-air craft above the landscape. Utterly exhilarating. Have you tried it?

DEREK: I'm acrophobic.

KEN: Scared of adjustable steel props?

DEREK: Heights. Sandra changes the lightbulbs.

KEN: Maybe not a good idea then. I've been on a few flights since, absolutely love it... even joined the British Balloon and Airship Club with the aim of getting my pilot's licence. That's quite a lengthy process, so in the meantime I've been carrying out some experiments in the garden... I thought it would be more difficult to get airborne, but it turns out all you need is a plastic garden chair, helium canister and some giant party balloons. Plus, a length of rope.

Enter SANDRA. She wheels a drinks trolley across the terrace.

KEN: I'll show you later.

SANDRA: *(to KEN)* I'm loving your posh bar cart.

KEN: It's the bar that goes far, Sandra... do you remember my half-brother Ed, the electronics boffin?

SANDRA: Lives in Australia?

KEN: That's him. He's trying to develop one which is voice-activated. Imagine it... the bar comes when you call. No need to get up.

SANDRA: You haven't anyway... *(hands KEN a large glass of water)* drink this please.

KEN: Where's Yvette?

SANDRA: Dropping off a bag of ribbons at the activities centre. George forgot them. They're marking out woodland trails for the children tomorrow. She won't be long.

KEN: I see.

SANDRA: *(refills their wine glasses)* Which means, we get the Chablis... *(sits)* how is Ed?

KEN: OK, when I last spoke to him. Still working for Samsung in Sydney.

SANDRA:	Still with… Scott, is it?
KEN:	Scott? No, they split up a while ago. That didn't end well. Scott went back to Canada. Not before he'd lost about twenty grand of Ed's money though.
SANDRA:	No?! Yvette never said anything. How did he manage that?
KEN:	An investment scam involving a new ski resort in the Northern Territory. A fantastic opportunity to get in right at the start.
DEREK:	It doesn't snow in the Northern Territory.
KEN:	Nobody told Scott… and Scott didn't think to check. Nice guy but thinking not one of his strong points. There was a subtle clue in the name of the development: Godron Mountain Resort… Godron is an anagram of drongo.
SANDRA:	Oh dear, poor Ed. That can't have been easy.
KEN:	No. I think once the disbelief and anger had worn off, he felt embarrassment

more than anything. Embarrassment that he spent two years of his life with someone who's got the IQ of a toothbrush... he's quite philosophical about the whole episode now, takes the view that he would never have met Matthew if it hadn't happened... Matthew works for the financial regulator in New South Wales. He was part of the state investigation team.

Pause

DEREK: *(to Sandra)* Was Benson inside with you?

SANDRA: No, you said he'd gone up the garden... *(DEREK looks blank)* when we first came out here. Lunch had just started.

DEREK: I don't think so, but our choice of beliefs is a personal matter. The important thing to focus on is our dog's current location. Which appears to be that field over there...

SANDRA: You'd better go and get him then.

DEREK: I'll do that, shall I? *(stands)* Don't get up, my love. No need to interrupt your enjoyment of the afternoon. No need at all... have you got the lead?

SANDRA:	Not on me, Derek, no. Try the kitchen table where you left it.

DEREK exits across the terrace and into the house.

ACT II

The setting is the same, sometime later. SANDRA and KEN sit at the table.

KEN:	You've never been banned?
SANDRA:	No! Have you?
KEN:	Ten years ago, for six months. When I had the TVR. Got done for speeding four times in the space of a year. I sold it afterwards... that car always reminds me of my friend Dom. We went to France in it for a boys' holiday. Did you ever meet him?
SANDRA:	I don't think so.
KEN:	My best mate, once upon a time. We were at college together. That trip down through France in the TVR was the last time I saw him... it's funny, the first time I encountered Dom was in a vehicle. I was eighteen years old at this

151

student party, with about a hundred other people and a bumper crop of magic mushrooms; the next thing I know, a bunch of us are piling into this battered VW camper.

SANDRA: To go somewhere?

KEN: To get pizza, obviously... the van was yellow, so it wasn't long before "Yellow Submarine" starts up. But because of the psilocybin, everyone becomes convinced we actually are beneath the waves. And then somebody notices we're being followed by a big, blue fish. Much to the amusement of the entire crew.

SANDRA: A big fish with four wheels and a blue light?

KEN: That type of fish. Our submarine comes to a stop and this policeman knocks on the window. Very slowly, the helmsman – who turned out to be Dom – winds it down and says to him with total conviction: "Sorry, Officer, but you have no jurisdiction underwater. Please return to the surface and resume your duties up there." Bit of a showstopper when that came out in court. Which is where Dom discovered the police actually pulled him over around two in the morning for driving down the middle of the road at ten miles an hour.

SANDRA: You're not in touch anymore?

KEN: Not for a long time. Last I heard he'd married a Danish woman and moved to Copenhagen. Very involved in environmental activism these days, according to his sister. Which is a bit unexpected – when I knew him, the only thing green about Dom was his complexion.

Pause

SANDRA: Top-up?

KEN: I think so.

SANDRA: *(pours)* That's the end of bottle two.

KEN: We need a waiter now.

Enter DEREK. He closes the door behind him and walks across the terrace.

DEREK   *(to SANDRA)* Right on cue.

SANDRA: *(to DEREK)* Did you get Benson?

DEREK: Eventually... *(sits)* I've put him inside. We need to keep that door shut. He was right by the road, miles over there... fortunately, Yvette drove past and picked us up.

KEN: Where is she now?

DEREK: Having a shower, I believe. She said she got roped into helping and wanted to freshen up.

KEN: Did she.

DEREK: How are you feeling, Kenneth?

KEN: Mysteriously better.

DEREK: Anything you'd like me to bring out here before our departure? Time marches on and we have no intention of overstaying our welcome...

SANDRA: What?

KEN: More wine...

SANDRA: We're not leaving yet, Derek... I've hardly seen my sister since we got here.

DEREK: I can't be blamed for that. Yvette chose to spend the afternoon somewhere else.

KEN: Good point.

SANDRA: I'm not blaming anyone... she was being helpful.

DEREK: We've only got her word for it.

SANDRA: What does that mean?

DEREK: She could have been anywhere. Pilates, poaching...

SANDRA: She hasn't been poaching.

DEREK: It's no more unlikely than taking a bag of ribbons to the woods.

KEN: *(to DEREK)* I like where you're going with this. What do you think we should do?

DEREK: Given her prolonged absence...

SANDRA: It wasn't prolonged.

DEREK: It would be reasonable to request corroborating evidence.

SANDRA:	Don't be ridiculous.

KEN:	Why not? You're willing to accept her story at face value; Derek clearly isn't. I respect that.

DEREK:	If Yvette's been setting up woodland trails as she claims, then you'd expect her to know certain details about them.

KEN:	You would... start time, length, duration, number of participants...

DEREK:	The kind of information a helper at such an event would naturally acquire... a series of simple questions should suffice. We can then compare her answers with those of the organiser, George.

KEN:	Brilliant!

SANDRA:	Absolutely not.

Enter YVETTE. She walks across the terrace and sits at the table.

YVETTE:	Sorry I've been so long.

SANDRA:	You haven't, don't worry... Ken's been entertaining us.

DEREK: That door needs to remain closed at all times.

YVETTE: What for?

DEREK: Your garden is not dog-proof.

YVETTE: It's nice to get fresh air in the house. Why don't you just tie the dog up out here?

DEREK: Benson doesn't like being tied up. He had a bad experience being left outside a buzzy boutique once. It traumatised him.

YVETTE: For God's sake. He's a dog.

SANDRA: *(gets up)* I'll close the door. I'm going inside anyway.

KEN: Don't forget the wine.

SANDRA: I'm ahead of you, Brother-In-Law.

SANDRA exits across the terrace and into the house, closes door behind her.

YVETTE: *(to DEREK)* You really need to stop treating that animal like it's got special needs. The more you indulge him, the more neurotic he's going to get.

KEN:	How were things at the activities centre?
YVETTE:	A bit manic but I think George has it under control.
KEN:	Isn't that great. Good for George.
YVETTE:	Sorry?
DEREK:	*(to YVETTE)* I'm interested in these trails through the woods. How many are there?
YVETTE:	Three or four, I think.

DEREK produces a notepad and pen, writes.

DEREK:	And what distance are they?
YVETTE:	I've got no idea, Derek. I haven't measured them… what are you doing?
DEREK:	*(writes)* When? Later today?
YVETTE:	Now. Are you writing down what I'm saying?
DEREK:	Not all of it, no. Neither of your last two questions, for example… if we could return to your previous answer, which

I found slightly unsatisfactory. There must be estimated completion times that would give an idea of distance?

YVETTE: Why are you writing down any of it?

DEREK: For the purposes of corroboration.

YVETTE: Corroboration of what?

DEREK: Your location this afternoon. I don't consider that unreasonable.

YVETTE: Sorry, let's get this straight. You want me to prove that I've been at the activities centre?

Pause

DEREK: Right, how about this? I'm going to Haverfordwest... *(gets up, walks round the table, sits)* sorry I've been so long.

YVETTE: You haven't. All you've done is walk round the table.

DEREK: That's not the point I'm trying to make. Imagine I said that's what I was doing before I left. Now I'm back.

YVETTE: OK. How was Haverfordwest?

DEREK: A bit manic.

DEREK waits for YVETTE to ask another question. She doesn't. Enter SANDRA.

SANDRA: I bring wine…

SANDRA closes the door, walks across the terrace to the table.

YVETTE: Thank God for that.

SANDRA: *(sits)* And some balloons I found.

KEN: Aha!

SANDRA: *(opens bag)* These are enormous.

KEN: A metre in diameter, fully inflated. We're going to need six of them, if my calculations are correct.

SANDRA: What for?

KEN: The test flight.

YVETTE: No, Ken. That's not a good idea.

KEN: Why not? The conditions are perfect, and we've got fully qualified ground crew present.

DEREK: There's sufficient helium for six of those balloons?

KEN: A full cannister of gas... specially selected plastic chair, rope, umbrella stand, sandbags. All the professional equipment needed for a controlled aeronautical experiment.

YVETTE: *(to KEN)* You can hardly walk... trying to fly in garden furniture is not a sensible option.

KEN: I know. And Derek's not good with heights.

Pause

SANDRA: Well, there's no way I'm volunteering.

YVETTE: Nor me.

KEN: Fair enough. In which case, we have a vacancy for a test pilot... the question is, do we know anyone who enjoys outdoor activities, owes us a favour and happens to be coming round anyway?

YVETTE: No, Ken. You can't expect...

ACT III

The setting is the same, sometime later. YVETTE and DEREK sit at the table.

YVETTE: I'm considering moving the garden path right over to the edge. And making it more sinuous. Ken always wanted a straight line down the middle, of course. The most direct route from one end of the lawn to the other. I don't like the way it seems to cut through the grass, like a motorway through countryside. Something meandering would be much more harmonious...

DEREK: *(points)* What colour would you call this umbrella?

YVETTE: Lavender.

DEREK: I'd say it was mauve.

DEREK gets up, looks around.

YVETTE: Going somewhere?

DEREK: I think I'll try sitting over there.

YVETTE: Alright.

DEREK walks round table, sits in a different chair.

YVETTE: How's that?

DEREK: Better.

YVETTE: The other idea I'm toying with is far more radical… giving the whole garden back to nature. Letting the lawn grow completely wild. Turn it into a meadow, with no paths or restrictions of any kind. Just seeing what happens. Wouldn't that be lovely? Full of different grasses, bees, flowers and butterflies. A haven for…

DEREK gets up.

YVETTE: Not good?

DEREK: No. Not at all.

DEREK walks round table, sits in another chair. Pause.

YVETTE: How's that working?

DEREK: A possibility.

YVETTE: Good… Ken's horrified by that plan. If he had his way, there'd be a swimming pool with paving round it. Perhaps a narrow strip of shaved grass at the sides. A large barbeque area, pizza oven and a bar all the way along the back. Essentially making the entire garden a kind of club area for entertaining... what's wrong?

DEREK: This isn't the right place.

YVETTE: Well, I don't know what to suggest. You've run out of options... *(realises DEREK is eyeing up her chair)* no.

DEREK: I haven't tried that one.

YVETTE: I'm sitting here.

Pause

DEREK: That's where I'd like to sit.

YVETTE: For God's sake... *(gets up)* have the bloody chair then.

YVETTE and DEREK swap places.

YVETTE: Happy now?

DEREK: This is the best position.

YVETTE: Actually, I think I prefer it over here... you're not looking at the back door of the house... there's a pretty view across the fields... it's facing the afternoon sun... yes, this is lovely. I don't know why I didn't sit here in the first place... we were talking about the garden, weren't we? I'm the one who does most of the work, so I don't see why I shouldn't have—

DEREK: *(points to the umbrella)* Lilac.

YVETTE: Maybe.

DEREK: Can I have my chair back?

YVETTE: No, you can't. I like it here.

Enter SANDRA and KEN.

SANDRA: *(speaking to KEN as they make their way over to the table)* You're getting the hang of that stick now.

KEN: There's a bit of a knack to it, like most things... *(to YVETTE)* what's happened to George?

YVETTE: Not sure... *(looks at her phone)* I sent him a text half an hour ago.

DEREK: Have you informed him about the test flight?

YVETTE: No!

KEN: You haven't?

YVETTE: No, I haven't. Alright?

DEREK: Is there anything you'd like to tell us? Now would be a good time.

YVETTE: I haven't mentioned the test flight to George. Is everybody clear about that? If I honestly thought it would bother him, I might. But I don't.

DEREK: You're not concealing anything?

YVETTE: No. Not that it's any of your business.

DEREK: In that case, are you prepared to submit your phone for examination?

SANDRA: *(to DEREK)* Stop.

YVETTE: No Derek, I'm definitely not.

DEREK: I'm going to need your phone, Yvette.

YVETTE: Forget it.

DEREK.   *(twitches)* If you won't give it to me, I'll have to take it.

YVETTE: I'm sorry?

SANDRA: *(to DEREK)* Don't.

DEREK: I need to see it right now. Pass it to me, please.

YVETTE: You're not having my phone, Derek. End of story.

DEREK: It's important you hand it over. I'm giving you one last chance.

YVETTE: No. I'm not giving you the phone.

Derek's right arm reaches over to snatch the phone; just in time, his left hand catches it by the wrist. He slaps his face.

DEREK: *(to himself)* Don't do that. Sorry…

SANDRA: STOP!

Pause. SANDRA counts to five. DEREK stares straight ahead, motionless. YVETTE and KEN exchange glances.

KEN: *(to DEREK)* Everything alright?

DEREK: I'm very well, thanks, Kenneth. I was just thinking how nice the garden looked. Especially the yellow roses… Yvette's handiwork, I believe.

KEN: Absolutely, every plant… I'm no gardener
                but I do have a good eye for design. A
                lot of people think so. And there's no
                doubt those trees would provide a lovely
                backdrop for a swimming pool.

YVETTE: A lot of people think so.

KEN: What?

SANDRA: *(to YVETTE)* The garden does look
                gorgeous. I hope it gets appreciated.
                Mine's been a lot of work this year…
                among other things, I got black spot on
                my roses.

YVETTE: That's a nightmare once it gets
                established. Did you spray in time?

SANDRA: I did. Mixed up some of Granny's
                remedy and doused them.

YVETTE: Thrice, as she taught us?

SANDRA: "You do this thrice, girls. Within one
                fortnight…" *(YVETTE'S phone beeps)*
                That might be George.

YVETTE: *(looks at her phone)* No, it's my local
                gossip group… breaking news, Ken. The
                police have arrested Maggie Barton.

KEN:	What for?
YVETTE:	*(reads)* On suspicion of making a false statement.
SANDRA:	Who's this?
YVETTE:	The landlady of The Chestnut Horse, one of the local pubs. Not one you'd want to visit.
KEN:	I don't know, there's something quite pleasingly medieval about the place. It's the kind of tavern where they have arm-wrestling and cockfighting.
YVETTE:	Lots of pub-kids running about while the parents get pissed.
DEREK:	That's a serious offence. Making a false statement to the police is not a trivial matter. It could lead to a charge of perverting the course of justice. And a custodial sentence, if convicted.
KEN:	*(to YVETTE)* What about the nephew?
YVETTE:	*(reads)* Rob Cowper is helping the police with their enquiries. He turned himself in after that boy in hospital slipped into a coma... had a crisis of conscience and

admitted being at the scene. Although not the actual attack.

KEN: Which means Aunt Maggie provided a false alibi for him. As you suspected.

YVETTE: Bit too convenient that Rob happened to be helping out in her pub all evening. The very night his ex's new boyfriend gets beaten up in town.

SANDRA: Who was responsible for the attack, according to Mr Cowper?

YVETTE: He claims it was a casual acquaintance. Can't remember his name.

DEREK: A murder charge might jog his memory.

YVETTE'S phone beeps again.

YVETTE: A reply, finally…

She reads the message, frowns.

SANDRA: Well, what does it say?

YVETTE: George won't be coming… he's with his wife.

KEN: He might need a drink after that.

YVETTE:	I don't think so... it sounds like they've had a rapprochement. Decided to give it another try, again... he's coming to collect his things after work tomorrow.
DEREK:	That's good news for Jonny.
YVETTE:	Sorry, I'm not with you. How does it possibly benefit him in any way, shape or form?
DEREK:	I was under the impression he wanted to move into the annex. George is now returning to the marital home which...
YVETTE:	Jonny doesn't want to move in there. It's the last thing he wants.
DEREK:	He's changed his mind? I suppose that's his prerogative... it's not a straightforward decision, by any means. There are good arguments for and against living in the annex.
KEN:	Bit of a shame we won't get to test out the flying chair... I'm pleased for George though, if they've managed to sort things out.
YVETTE:	(*gets up*) I think I'd like a glass of wine.

YVETTE exits across the terrace and into the house.

DEREK: *(calls)* DOOR!

The door slams shut.

DEREK: It would be interesting to know Rebecca's view on the subject.

KEN: Becca? Why would she have an opinion? It's none of her concern.

Pause

DEREK: Sandra's right, you have got some feudal beliefs.

KEN: I'm sorry?

SANDRA: *(to DEREK)* I think now might be a good moment for us to head off.

DEREK: Ready when you are, my love.

SANDRA: You need to stop obsessing about the annex. It doesn't affect you in the slightest.

Enter YVETTE. She walks across the terrace to the table. SANDRA gets up and closes the door.

YVETTE:	Here we go… *(pours herself a large glass)* anyone else?
KEN:	I'll join you.
SANDRA:	We should probably be getting back…
YVETTE:	*(fills SANDRA'S glass)* Just a small one.
KEN:	So, Sandra, my favourite sister-in-law… which of my beliefs would you call feudal?
YVETTE:	Only sister-in-law. *(sits)* All of them, I imagine.
SANDRA:	I didn't actually put it quite—
DEREK:	How about your view that it's not the woman's concern where a couple lives, Kenneth?
KEN:	What?
YVETTE:	Yup, that's one of them.
KEN:	No, it isn't.
YVETTE:	It certainly was when we moved here twenty-five years ago. I don't suppose you feel differently now.

KEN:	Hang on a minute. It was a joint decision to move.
YVETTE	It was. Between you and the accountant... all those juicy grants available at the time to relocate a business to Wales.
SANDRA:	*(to YVETTE)* It worked out well though, didn't it? You've always said how much you love this part of the world.
YVETTE:	I do – this is home. We've got lots of friends and it's been a wonderful place to bring up children. But that doesn't alter the fact I didn't have much say in the matter before it happened.
KEN:	Bollocks. I remember you getting very excited about property prices compared to London.
YVETTE:	It was presented to me as a fait accompli, not a possibility to be discussed between us.
KEN:	A bit like George moving into the annex.
DEREK:	Is there any cheese left?

YVETTE: What's that got to do with anything?

SANDRA: There's some Red Leicester, I think.

KEN: That's what this is about…

DEREK: It was more the Gorgonzola I was after.

YVETTE: Christ you're pathetic. You're actually jealous.

SANDRA: All gone. There might be a bit of Brie, unless someone ate that too.

KEN: Me? At least try and hide your disappointment he's back with his wife.

DEREK: I could actually do with something sweet. Are we going to get dessert?

YVETTE: How dare you! Don't project your sordid insecurities onto me.

SANDRA: No. Lunch is over.

TEN

For reasons he didn't entirely comprehend, Mr Tile was aware that his wife seemed to hold him directly responsible for the volcanic argument which erupted chez Yvette et Ken prior to their departure; that somehow, he had manipulated the gaseous pressure, silica content, volume and buoyancy of the marital magma.

"A moron blundering socially inept" had been the charge furiously levelled against him as soon as the Jag got clear of the drive, and it was possible his objection to this grammatical anarchism didn't endear him to the presiding magistrate. The judgement had been summary; the sentence Sandra's silence. The kind of silence where polar bears roam, that other cultures cut into blocks and use to build igloos; the kind which can stand for millennia in towering majesty and laughs in the face of a half-hour hop between Haverfordwest and Carmarthen on the A40.

While The One Who Chooses Not To Speak stared out of the passenger window, watching two swallows swoop and harry each other like fighter planes in an old war film, Derek considered his three options:

1. Accept culpability without qualification. Or understanding.
2. Calmly suggest there may have been a problem before their arrival. A problem that was manifestly present, even though he never came.
3. Point out an irresistibly fascinating feature on the driver's side along the route, thereby tempting her to turn towards him.

He cleared his throat. 'There's an unusual garage coming up on the right. I noticed it on the way. If you have a look at the pumps, it would appear they only sell diesel—'

'Pull over, please.'

'Everything OK, my love?'

'I need some air.'

Mrs Tile got out of the car the moment it came to a stop in the lay-by, opened the back door and picked up the lead. She looked at Benson. 'Come on.'

'Are we going for a walk?'

'Some of us are... no prizes for guessing what you're doing.'

'Will you be long?'

'Five minutes.'

Interestingly, the available data indicated this was in fact the median PWT. Knowing this gave an AWT nearer twenty minutes, Mr Tile removed his leather gloves finger by finger, reached into the driver's map pocket, or DSC (Door Storage Compartment) as he preferred to call it on the basis of descriptive accuracy, and pulled out his book.

Sandra walked away from the road and through a small copse of beech trees, joining a track that followed the side of a high hedgerow towards a wooden gate. As she approached, there was a sudden glimpse of simmering poppies in open fields with woodland rising behind; a bubbling red foam to complement the cooler green tones in the colour palette of this luminous landscape.

On the other side of the gate, on a camping chair with a sketch pad on his lap, sat a figure she recognised; nearby, a woman lay asleep on a rug. Benson also remembered The Man Who Gives Carrots and wandered up to him hopefully, his tail wagging. 'Hello, mate,' Barry greeted the dog.

Sandra leaned over his shoulder to appraise the picture. 'Not bad.'

He glanced at his sleeping companion and lowered his voice conspiratorially. 'I've been encouraged to dive into the waters of my creativity.'

'How's that working for you?'

'I've decided drawing's not my thing, Sandra. Having done some diving, it turns out the depth of my talent is more pond than Pacific.'

'Who's your friend?'

'Erika, from Denmark. We met on the beach that evening after your visit. She thinks we were married in a former life.'

'Were you?'

Barry considered the idea. 'It's possible. To be honest, there are long periods when I don't really remember much.'

'Did you read her your poetry in the living room?'

'I did. And it had a significantly more seductive effect than on you.'

'Maybe the firelight helped.' Sandra looked around. 'Where's all your stuff?'

'Erika's got a camper van. We're driving up to Liverpool tomorrow, then catching a ferry over to Ireland. We're going to travel about for a bit. Be a nice change doing it in comfort; I'm fed up with walking.' He reached into his bag. 'In case you're feeling left out and starved of my attention, I've written something else you might like…' Barry opened his notebook and started reading aloud before Sandra had a chance to react. 'This one's called "The Good Man":

'In a small town lived a good man.
He'd been single for a long time
and no one invited him to parties.
Next door lived a bad man.
He had a beautiful girlfriend
and a wide circle of friends.
One evening they met on the street.
"Tell me where I'm going wrong, Neighbour,"
the good man asked the bad.
"Every day I try to do a good deed,
and they say virtue is its own reward.
But to be totally honest,
I'd like some other benefits as well."
"If you want to be a winner like me,"
the bad man replied,
"popular and a success with the ladies,
then you need to do something dramatic.
Make a bit of a name for yourself,
that's what everyone loves.

Meet me outside the school
at ten tomorrow morning.
Bring a can of petrol and some matches."
They met as arranged the next day
and the bad man explained the plan.
The good man was to start a fire,
wait exactly ten minutes,
then raise the alarm and take the credit
for saving all the children.
The good man eagerly accepted,
thinking of the glory that awaited him,
and crept behind the building.
Exactly five minutes later,
the bad man ran into the school.
He rushed from room to room
warning about the flames he'd seen
licking at the windows
from outside on the road.
Then stole all the laptops
when the place was empty.
One man was caught red-handed,
arrested and charged with arson.
He spent a long time in prison.
The other was hailed as a hero
and given an award for bravery.
He took his girlfriend to Turkey
with the money that he made
from the sale of some computers.
Everyone agreed that he deserved
a nice holiday in the sun.'

As they were saying goodbye, Barry asked if Sandra had any travel tips about Ireland; she thought for a moment. 'If you're in County Galway, then it's worth making a detour to see The Home of the Oranmore Hermit. I'd highly recommend a visit.' Mrs Tile smiled to herself as she walked along the narrow footpath at the side of the poppy field.

To cheer himself up, Derek turned to a short chapter towards the end of *Noteworthy Felonies in the County of Berkshire*; the story amused him, even though his enjoyment was of the undemonstrative variety. He always found it slightly strange to witness other people laughing out loud and couldn't quite decide if he was missing something or they were, the hysteria indicating a vitamin deficiency like rickets. A connection which could perhaps explain the peculiar idiom "funny bone".

One afternoon in September 1848, a young gentleman arrived at Reading railway station carrying a small suitcase. He walked the short distance across town to The Grand Hotel, where he requested a room and a table for dinner at 20:00. Dressed somewhat carelessly, though in clothes of the finest quality, the visitor was polite, if taciturn, and pleasantly well spoken. However, there was an unmistakable sadness about his demeanour, a withdrawn and distracted melancholy that clearly signalled a state of depression. The gentleman's name was Matthew Scott, a conman who would be transported to Australia by spring of the following year.

At 20:30 that evening, when Mr Scott had failed to appear in the restaurant, a member of staff was dispatched to his room. The waiter found the door ajar and the guest lying on his bed in a distressed condition; clutching an empty bottle of opium tincture in one hand and a short note in the other, Matthew asked that a priest be sent for immediately. The startled employee rushed downstairs to the hotel manager's office and reported what he'd encountered: attempted suicide by laudanum overdose. A doctor was hastily summoned, emetics administered and a nurse stationed by the patient's bedside for the night.

By the next morning, news of this tragic event had spread throughout the building, prompting concern and sympathy in equal measure. Quick to spot the chance for some favourable publicity, and keen to burnish The Grand's reputation as an establishment that operated in a class apart, the manager announced at breakfast that poor Mr Scott would be staying free of charge until he was fully restored to health, that all guests were regarded as members of the family during their stay and if one of them needed help then they could expect to be treated accordingly. A speech which generated prolonged applause and a spate of repeat bookings.

During the first day, details slowly began to emerge about the cause of Matthew's despair: in just the last month, he had been swindled out of most of his inheritance by a confidence trickster – French, it was rumoured – and left in much reduced circumstances; then his beloved fiancée, rather than console and comfort him, had bluntly broken off their engagement as a consequence. Now broken-hearted and considerably poorer, he had simply lost all faith in human nature and any will to live.

This moving story of betrayal and loss touched the sensibilities of men and women alike, appealing as it did to the contemporary taste for melodrama, and very soon the trickle of well-wishers to the celebrity victim's room became a torrent, such that, taking personal control of the situation in the best interests of Mr Scott, the manager organised a queueing system in the corridor outside with a selection of refreshments available to purchase. Who originally came up with the idea for a recovery fund is unclear, but the use of a small suitcase propped open against the sickbed as a collection box, carefully positioned to be visible from both the pillow and door, combined with the remarkable similarity in handwriting between the suicide note and the sign – "We beseech all Christian brethren to give what each can spare that one of our own might be restored to life" – located in the lid of the case, provided some clues had anyone been looking. The scheme was certainly effective. In a fever of competitive compassion, driven by a genuine desire to provide philanthropic assistance for the unfortunate, and an equally genuine desire not to be outdone in displays of public generosity, this stream of Good Samaritans poured money into Matthew's recovery over the following week.

It came as no surprise to those guests who had expertise in such matters (all of them), or to those who had suffered some comparable misfortune (most of them) and eagerly awaited the latest progress bulletin to confirm their (previously unverbalised) predictions, that the path to good health proved arduous and uneven. It was not until the second day that Mr Scott was persuaded to try a little food; on the third he managed slightly more sustenance and even some wine, much to the delight of onlookers. On the evening of the fourth day, Matthew felt well enough to eat in the restaurant, where he received a standing ovation and numerous gifts from his fellow diners, so many, in fact, that a porter had to help him carry several bottles back to his room at midnight. Unfortunately, on the morning of the fifth, he suffered a relapse in his depression and was unable to leave his bed for the entire day. By the afternoon of the sixth, Mr Scott's good spirits had been revived after a lengthy luncheon, much to the relief of the hotel manager, whose feelings of kinship were starting to fade, a fact not entirely lost on the convalescent. Finally, on the seventh day, his strength returned and faith in mankind renewed, Matthew departed the premises to cheers and tears, a grateful smile on his face and a tidy sum in his case. Nearly forty-six pounds the fund amounted to when he'd counted the donations in private that morning, equating to about five thousand six hundred today, Derek calculated.

Mr Scott headed straight to a bank, and then to the railway station. He alighted from the train at Windsor and walked the short distance across town to The Royal Hotel; once there, he requested a room and a table for dinner at 20:00. The curtain went up shortly after 20:30 and the performance started again.

His luck ran out seven weeks later in November 1848 at The Imperial Hotel, Bracknell. The same waiter who came to find him that first evening at The Grand had moved jobs to the restaurant of this establishment just days before Matthew's arrival. If the con artist had chosen to stay somewhere else, or gone to Bracknell sooner after leaving Reading, he might never have been caught; unsurprisingly, The Imperial's new member of staff recognised him at once. When the authorities searched his room, they discovered a diary among his possessions in which he recorded the details of his fraud: places, dates and the exact sum deposited in the bank afterwards. As well as Reading, Windsor and Bracknell, Mr Scott had attempted suicide in Maidenhead, Sandhurst, Crowthorne, Twyford and Ascot. Income from his autumn tour of Berkshire totalled two hundred and ninety-six pounds; expenditure comprised little more than a few train tickets. He was transported to Australia in March 1849 and settled in Melbourne when he'd served his four-year sentence.

Matthew went into the retail business and used his eye for an opportunity to make a fortune selling snowshoes, ice picks and other polar essentials to prospectors travelling from the city to the Northern Territory during the 1856 gold rush. He married Helen Foster, the daughter of a respected local hotelier, later the same year and they had two sons, William and Ralph. In 1880, the young siblings travelled to America together where they encountered a new kind of light, effervescent beer imported from Northern Europe, known as lager. On their return to Melbourne from New York, assisted to a degree by family investment, the brothers founded a small brewery. The new venture was called after their mother's maiden name.

Mr Tile had been dozing, having a strange dream in which laudanum, lager and luck figured prominently, when the rear passenger door of the Jag opened and Benson jumped onto his travel rug. Without a word, Sandra filled the 3C (Collapsible Canine Container) with water, closed the back and got in the front. She settled herself in the seat, then turned to look at her husband. 'Now, shall we try and make the rest of the journey pleasant?' Rhetorical genius, Derek had to admit. But the use of that first person plural wasn't fooling anyone. This simple question contained checkmate in three moves:

1. He'd been responsible for any unpleasantness up to that point.
2. Any unpleasantness from that point on was his responsibility.
3. Disputing either of the above would create unpleasantness for which he'd be responsible.

Mr Tile picked up his leather driving gloves from the dashboard and pulled them on finger by finger. 'We shall, my love.'

*

Two months later, at a festival in County Galway where he was working, Erika would encourage Barry to try his luck at a spoken word event. He was to prove an instant hit, receiving rapturous applause, invitations to perform elsewhere and (less welcome to his new manager) several offers of marriage. His poem "Sandra", about a woman's unrequited love for a traveller she meets, would feature in a highlights programme for Irish radio. He never visited The Home of the Oranmore Hermit.

ELEVEN

Their table was taken. That was the unpalatable fact which presented itself as they rounded the corner of the restaurant for dinner at 19:30 sharp. A man of about fifty, dressed in smart-casual chinos, shirt and jacket, was sitting in Sandra's chair studying the menu. No debate took place among the members of Team Tile. Almost without breaking stride, Derek led the way across the terrace to confront the furniture usurper and recover what was rightfully theirs.

The man looked up. 'Ah, good. A bottle of Sancerre, and could you tell me what the fish of the day is?'

'I don't work here.'

The interloper seemed surprised. 'No? What do you want then?'

'There's been a mistake. This table is reserved.'

The hint of a smile played across the encroacher's lips. 'Really?' His face was a picture of innocence. 'Who's the reservation for?'

'Us,' Mr Tile replied, assuming that would be the end of the matter.

'Oh no, surely not. How terrible. We can't have that.'

'It's unfortunate, I agree.'

'Let's be clear… this is your table which you've reserved and here you are wanting to sit at your table which you've reserved, only to find I'm sitting here because this is the table I was offered when I arrived before you.'

'That was the mistake.'

Mr Trespass shook his head. 'Dear me, what's wrong with the world? If only things would always go exactly the way we wanted.' He tutted. 'That must've been a nasty shock when you arrived expecting to spend the evening at this table and saw someone else had got there first.'

Derek glanced at his wife. 'It was.'

'Had it all planned out, I bet. A nice meal in the hotel restaurant, sitting in the perfect spot… and to think I've only just got here myself. Can't be more than a few minutes ago. Just imagine, if I'd chosen to go so somewhere else, or you'd arrived a bit sooner, this wouldn't have happened. You'd sitting here right now, not me… unfortunately, you're too late. And that's not my problem, I'm afraid.'

'I'm going to find Will,' Sandra informed her husband. She headed towards the bar area at the front, passing a black-haired woman wearing a summer dress decorated with a yellow-rose print coming the other way. The owner of the floral dress walked towards the scene of the (escalating) dispute but paused when she caught sight of Derek; she lingered close enough to listen to the conversation.

'This is our table,' Mr Tile asserted.

'It's not yours. It belongs to the hotel… unless I'm mistaken and you brought the table with you.'

'We reserved it for the duration of our stay when we first arrived. Which predates any claim you may have by two whole days. According to your own logic, the right thing is for you to move.'

The space invader laughed. 'Listen, Beard Boy, I'm not going anywhere.' He stood up and extended an arm towards the woman hovering behind Mr Tile. 'Now, perhaps you'd be kind enough to piss off so we can have dinner…'

Sandra found her husband standing motionless in the middle of the restaurant, staring straight ahead. 'Will's not working this weekend,' she told him. 'He forgot to pass on our reservation. It's been sorted out but there's nothing they can do tonight. I've ordered takeaway fish and chips. We don't want to stay here.'

They ate in silence on a bench overlooking the bay with the beach laid out beneath them at low tide like a polished travertine slab of swirling, patterned formations. A plan would emerge in due course; there was no need for any discussion. Whatever it brought, the Tiles knew tomorrow promised to be a busy day.

In fact, the ball started rolling before they made it to bed that night. Derek was performing the last security checks in the squirrel-red dressing gown he'd taken to wearing with nothing underneath, offering unsolicited and unwelcome glimpses of certain furry fauna to other denizens of the caravan (both conjugal and canine), when there was a knock at the door. He opened it to find a woman he recognised standing outside, a shawl wrapped around her rose-print dress. 'My name's Gail. You might remember me from the restaurant. Sorry to disturb you like this… can I come in?'

Derek notified his wife that they had company then changed, on her instructions, into alternative loungewear "less reminiscent of late-stage Hugh Hefner", as she put it. Sandra was unimpressed at being interrupted in the bathroom, doubly so when she discovered the identity of their visitor.

'I'd like to apologise for Bruce,' Gail began. 'His behaviour earlier was appalling and there's absolutely no excuse for talking—'

'Your husband's one of the vilest people I've ever met,' Mrs Tile interrupted.

'Bruce isn't my husband. I am married but not to him… he's been divorced for a long time.'

Derek had some trouble computing these three pieces of information and her reasons for volunteering them so readily late at night on the sofa in their caravan. A number of possibilities occurred to him, none of them healthy, convenient or socially appropriate. He coughed. 'Can I ask what you're doing with him then?'

Gail lowered her head and took a deep breath. 'Essentially, being blackmailed into sex. He's got proof… I made a mistake. A big one. We had a brief fling, but he won't accept that's all it was… my problem is I love my husband.' She gazed at the floor and absently curled her hair. Then stopped. 'That's why I need your help.'

Sandra was staring intently. 'How exactly?'

'Bruce is a monster.' She looked at Derek. 'Like that dog.'

There was silence for a moment. Sandra leaned forward; she'd noticed something the visitor was wearing. 'Your necklace is lovely.'

'Thank you. I bought it the other day.' Gail held up the pendant for her to see. 'It's amber.'

'I thought so.' She turned and spoke to her husband with total conviction in her voice. 'This is what the hare knew. It's why we came here.'

An hour later, Mrs Tile seemed satisfied that she had sufficient material to be getting on with and announced she needed to meditate, to marinate the ingredients overnight. Crucially, there appeared to be a window of opportunity sometime the following afternoon; with the "what" and "why" settled, the elements left to decide were "how", "where" and exactly "when" – the meat of the matter. It was agreed that Gail would knock on their door again during her pre-breakfast run the next day.

At this point, to Derek's considerable alarm, the conversation took a sinister turn. A sense of foreboding gripped him as the discussion entered a darker realm, venturing into territory that made him physically uncomfortable. Apropos of nothing, as far as he could tell, Sandra asked Gail about the purchase of her jewellery. 'Did you say that you got the necklace recently?'

'On Wednesday. I came across this shop with some gorgeous pieces, completely by chance.'

'I do like that pendant.'

'The prices weren't ridiculous either... lots of things I could have bought in there.'

'Was it nearby?'

'Llangarloc... have you been? It's a really buzzy little place, full of independent boutiques and lovely...'

He decided it was time to go to bed.

The next morning, Derek found Sandra sitting at the kitchen table with various items laid out in front of her, none of them related to the preparation of a lavish weekend breakfast. 'You're up early, Mrs Tile.'

'Since five...' She sighed and shook her head. 'We need two boats this afternoon.'

Possibly because he'd just got out of bed, and had yet to perform the series of procedures that would render his brain fully operational, Mr Tile failed to comprehend why the hiring of a second vessel was strictly necessary. 'No need to fret, my love. I'm sure there will be ample opportunity for us both to have a turn at driving. We've purchased a two-hour slot on the water.'

His wife's mellifluous tone indicated that he'd been guilty of an ISI (Infuriating Spousal Idiocy). 'Not for us! Going out separately would be very odd. And immediately draw attention to us... I'm not going to talk to you again until you've had some coffee.'

Halfway through the mug, Derek judged that he was sufficiently awake to at least fake the role of ACE (Able Conversational Equal) and sat down. The model maker explained the land and seascape of the tabletop, whose topography had been formed entirely from pieces of travel backgammon. All thirty of the playing counters had been utilised in a string – with alternate colours, he noted approvingly – to shape the outline of Rhos Cove and the immediate coastline; a dice shaker, positioned in the sea beyond the bay, had become the Mew Stone; Gail and Bruce, represented by black and white dice respectively, were sitting on the beach; and the doubling dice, moored up further along the shore, was their rental boat and its crew.

He pointed to the salt and pepper cellars. 'What are those?'
'Condiments for food.'

Patiently, she ran through the reasons Rhos Cove had been selected as the preferred location. There were four:

1. The inlet was accessible by land but only on foot, not in a car.
2. It had a small beach with a mixture of shingle and larger pebbles, making it much less attractive to day trippers than the expanses of golden sand nearby.
3. That section of the coast path was temporarily closed, as they discovered on their walk three days ago. This meant the bay and area of sea just outside it had effectively become blind spots from the surrounding headlands. Nobody would be able to see them without being visible themselves, either on the beach or in a boat.
4. The Mew Stone made an obvious goal for competent swimmers; if Gail challenged him, the competitive Bruce wouldn't be able to resist.

This represented a masterpiece of strategic planning in Mr Tiles' opinion, worthy of the civil engineer Sir James Drake, designer of the Preston bypass in 1958 (now part of the M6), and generally regarded as the pioneer of Britain's motorway network. He told her as much, which elicited the first (half) smile of the morning. 'High praise indeed... there's only one problem: my scheme relies on two boats. I've tried, but it doesn't work otherwise. I'll show you.' She picked up the three dice and moved them round the coast. 'We'll start at quarter to two this afternoon.' Derek nodded and took his turn in the game, lifting the pepper into position next to the dice. Sandra glared at him. 'What are you doing?'

'Making the hotel.'

'Don't touch anything on the table again. I've been working on this for three hours.' She allowed the gravity of his offence to sink in, then continued. 'We go down to collect our boat for the start of the rental period at two o'clock. About the same time Gail and Bruce start walking. Which means all of us should be in situ,' she placed the dice back in Rhos Cove, 'around two-thirty ish. Simultaneously, the second boat takes up position out here,' she put the other white dice from the backgammon set next to the shaker, 'giving it a good view of any traffic in both directions.'

Mr Tile seized his chance. 'You've already used one of those for Bruce.' Before his wife could object, he removed the dice and replaced it with the salt. 'Less confusing, semiotically.'

She looked at him without affection. 'Congratulations.'

It transpired Gail had another job to do once she'd got Bruce to the bay: suggest a race out to the Mew Stone and let him win, by a distance; the important thing was that he swam out into the open water where the current would carry his body down the coast. Sandra moved Bruce in front of the dice shaker and Gail to the entrance of the inlet. 'We'll pick her up there and get her back to the beach as fast as possible.' The doubling dice left its mooring, collected the black and retuned to shore. 'When no one's anywhere near, the second boat speeds round like this...' She gripped the salt cellar and rammed it straight into the white dice, knocking the small cube out of the way. 'Then just carries on.' The salt disappeared out to sea across the table. 'After we've dropped Gail, our only concern is getting back to the hire place by four o'clock. Meanwhile, she goes to sleep sunbathing and at some point, not too soon, wakes up to find Bruce isn't there. Maybe he's gone for a walk. She looks but can't find him. Maybe he never returned from his swim. She has no idea. Phoning the hotel on the off-chance he went back to the room might be clever. But that's up to her. From this moment,' Sandra moved the doubling dice out of Rhos Cove, 'she's by herself. We'll never have any contact again.'

'Approaching perfection, my love.' He meant it.

'Approaching but sadly having to turn back at the last minute because there's a fatal flaw. Shame, I think it would work too... Gail will be here in a minute. We'll have to try and come up with something else. Could you put the kettle on?'

At the kitchen sink, Derek pulled up the blind to have a look at the morning – it was bright and beautiful already. While waiting for the water to boil, he gazed out of the window, his eyes resting on the small patch of grass where he'd killed the great canine creature forty-eight hours before. He thought of something and turned round. 'Today's Saturday, isn't it?' Luckily, there were many things he liked about his wife, one of them being that she never replied to this sort of question with "all day".

'Does that make a difference?'

'It might.'

'How?' There was a knock on the door. 'That's her... what do you want to do? Talk to me please.'

He made a decision. 'We go ahead with your plan. I know a way to get the second boat.'

Mrs Tile opened the door, and the yellow-jacket-wearer came inside.

When Gail left, fully briefed on her role and what to expect, although not apprised of those unknown parameters and random variables within the information matrix that didn't concern her, as Derek made clear, for reasons of mission security and her own protection, the Tiles went for a cooked breakfast. Special dispensation was granted, given the circumstances. And the fact Sandra was starving. After their calorie carnival, she went back to bed and her husband paid a visit to the neighbouring caravan.

The door opened immediately on this occasion. 'Greetings, fellow holidaymaker!' he began in his friendliest manner.

Kay's salutation was less effusive. 'Not you again... the caff's closed.'

'I was wondering the anticipated time of Lee's return today?'

'Why?'

Derek had a sense of déjà vu. 'Why do I want to know?'

'No. Why are you on our doorstep again?'

'I've just told you.'

She folded her arms. 'I don't believe you.'

'Can I ask why not?'

'Because it's not true.'

Mr Tile found himself in a familiar position: standing outside Number Nine being led down a conversational cul-de-sac. 'Yes, it is.'

She shook her head. 'You're after something else.'

He didn't know how to proceed. 'Sorry, maybe I haven't made myself clear...'

'Don't worry, I reckon it's very clear what your game is.'

'What game?'

Kay looked him up and down. 'You've come round to try it on before my boyfriend gets back. Wondering if there's enough time.'

'No, I haven't.'

'Hoping I might invite you in. Next thing it's all about how your wife doesn't understand you. Then, if I'm a lucky lady, I might get to stroke the head of your tortoise.' For the second time in her presence, Derek was too dumbfounded to speak. Kay screamed with laughter. 'Oh my god, that is fucking priceless… the look on your face!' She took several deep breaths and wiped her eyes. 'You are such a laugh mate. I'll give you that…' She started again. 'Stop it. I can't look at you… Lee's on the road – I'll let him know you came over.'

'Thank you.'

'Do call again,' she said in a strange voice.

The door closed and Mr Tile heard another scream of laughter as he walked away, his dearest wish being that he would never have cause to call again.

*

Eight months later, following her acrimonious break-up with Lee (he wanted another dog, she didn't), Kay would meet a man at a party called Jack Jones who made her laugh. She wasn't aware on the night of their romantic encounter, or for some time afterwards, that his family owned a large holiday park on the coast. One day, they would run this business together, with Kay operating the customer service side (including on-site facilities such as the café) on one guiding principle: the customer is always wrong.

*

While waiting for the kettle to boil, a conversation on Thursday afternoon had come back to him. Derek remembered mentioning to Lee that earlier he'd seen a jogger, a usefully gender-neutral noun that would add veracity to his story. The hope (in truth, the expectation) was that he could convince JJ's owner to participate in the maritime masterplan by combining elements of fact and fiction in chronological order. Mr Tile intended to impart three key pieces of information in his pitch, the results of a brainstorming session over breakfast. The last part would be true, the second mostly true and the first not quite true:

1. His wife saw a man in jogging kit feeding the dog something before they went for breakfast that fateful morning. She noticed his jacket was torn. By the time she realised the importance of this event, Lee had already left for Staines.
2. Sandra recognised the jogger in the restaurant last night. Their table reservation had got mixed up and this same man had been unnecessarily unpleasant.
3. The woman he'd been having dinner with came to their caravan to apologise afterwards. She revealed that this man, called Bruce, was blackmailing her and asked for help.

Details and elaborations could be supplied on demand as necessary. It seemed to Derek and Sandra that any reasonable person of sound mind, let alone the owner of the dead dog, would have little trouble justifying the termination of Bruce's oxygen contract. In fact, they'd overprepared if anything. When Lee heard part one, and the first sentence of part two, he needed no further encouragement to exact violent revenge; whether this provided evidence of reason and mind-soundness on his part wasn't something the Tiles ever discussed. The eyewitness account, confirming his own suspicions, and the perpetrator's continued presence in the hotel, blithely enjoying dinner in the restaurant as if nothing had happened, provided all the grounds he needed. It also correlated with the preliminary findings of the post-mortem: the dog's demise was consistent with the ingestion of a currently unknown substance, causing excessive sedation and depressed respiratory function which progressed rapidly to coma and death; put in layman's terms, the vet explained, JJ ate something, then fell into a sleep so deep his breathing stopped.

Not only was Lee pathologically motivated to seek waterborne retribution, but he provided the solution to a problem that hadn't even occurred to the Tiles: a pair of kids' walkie-talkies. Kay's eight-year-old son had brought his prize possessions on holiday with him, thereby facilitating a secure, untraceable telecoms channel between the two boats.

In the event, obtaining a second vessel had been less straightforward than envisaged, and the enterprise nearly fell apart on the jetty of the rental facility. Derek was lying on the sofa reading when Lee banged on the caravan window soon after arriving back; they'd sat at the table outside, where Lee remarked on the manifest benefits of the enhanced privacy afforded by Number Ten's sequential position at the terminus of the sward (or words to that effect, Mr Tile claimed later to his wife), then listened to the case against Bruce, and the planned redress, with surprising composure. After being shown the Mew Stone's exact location outside Rhos Cove on the map, he went straight to hire a boat when the meeting was finished, only to be told there were none available. A block booking for a blokes' fishing trip that afternoon had filled all the remaining slots, which meant he couldn't help: 'No can do today,' the boatman informed him bluntly. It was only when they got talking and Lee explained his intention – to scatter JJ's ashes at sea before he left – that the man's manner changed dramatically. He became quite emotional remembering his beloved dog Molly: the wonderful years they'd had together, the devotion and unconditional loyalty she'd always shown; how gently, with such great care, she took any food from his fingers; the heartbreak he'd suffered on her passing, a grief almost too terrible to bear; how he'd cradled her in death like when she was a pup and performed the same solitary ceremony on the water for Molly only three months before. The upshot was, the boatman offered Lee his own boat free of charge; they agreed on a time shortly after the changeover at 14:00.

This man's generosity turned out to be a stroke of good fortune in more ways than one: not only was the scheme able to go ahead, and Lee observe the aquatic ritual he wanted afterwards, but when the police forensic team examined the fleet of rental boats on Sunday (which they did in a particularly aggressive manner, as if the boatman was somehow responsible) as part of their investigation, they found no evidence of collision damage on any. Had they inspected another craft, belonging to the hire operator himself, they might have discovered a telltale dent in the hull, just below the waterline on the starboard bow, containing tiny particles of blood, skin, hair and bone. But they didn't.

(Question: 'Did you use the boat in the afternoon?' Truthful answer: 'No, I did not.')

Lying on his back in the privacy of the dunes behind his shack, preparing himself for the confrontation to come, Leonard tried to clear his mind. There were times when he had strange, restless moods and couldn't sleep at night. He would sit outside in the darkness listening to the gale blowing inside his head, thinking of all the millions across the millennia who had gone before. There is no meaning, the wind seemed to whisper, no meaning at all... he needed to pull himself together. This was not a moment for weakness or undiagnosed mental health issues; this was a moment for action, of the most direct kind. Today, of all days, he had to dig deep. The townsfolk required their lifeguard to be strong, to be a rock in this time of crisis, to stand up and show he was worthy of the name, of the respect he was awarded.

They were good people, who looked out for each other, especially the elderly and vulnerable. (Leonard himself had a strong sense of civic duty and liked to do his bit, giving regular evening talks at the care home on subjects as diverse as the red squirrel, life-

saving techniques and data analytics, which were always well attended by serene, smiley residents in the television lounge.) Unsophisticated, maybe; untravelled, perhaps. Some had never been as far as London, let alone experienced the exotic culture of a distant island like Madeira. Most had limited French. But in their hearts resided a simple integrity and decency that Leonard knew to be precious and all too rare in this dangerous world. Now the time had come for the lifeguard to prove he deserved to live amongst them as a trusted neighbour. This was the hour of reckoning; there could be no delay, evasion or excuse.

The gauntlet had been thrown down in no uncertain terms – a planning application had been lodged with the council to turn the waters of Culvermead Bay into an industrial fish farm. The scheme had been rejected, unanimously, after unprecedented local opposition which united not just the members of this community but many others along the coast who would be adversely affected by the proposal. But to no avail. An immediate appeal had been lodged and work started regardless; huge cages had appeared along the shore; hired thugs patrolled the long pontoons stretching across the bay like surgical incisions.

One man was responsible for this illegal outrage, one man with a long history of environmental desecration, animal cruelty and contempt for the wishes or welfare of anyone but himself. One man who had been a thorn in the side of Leonard and the people he loved for far too long. The kind of man who believed he could do as he pleased, behave as he liked, take any table he wanted in a restaurant, for example, with total impunity. Today that man was in for a shock, the shock of his life. The time for consequences had arrived. That man's name was Norfolk the Bruce.

TWELVE

At 13:45 exactly, the Tiles locked the caravan door, leaving Benson with a biscuit-flavoured bribe on the living room sofa – this was definitely not a dog-friendly expedition – and walked down the meadow past Number Nine. In the window, Lee acknowledged them with a brief nod; he would follow in twenty minutes as arranged. Derek was dressed in his superhero costume of red trunks and yellow T-shirt (in case of plan B), with the adventure gilet over the top; to his delight (he was starting to suspect she wasn't keen on the item), and for the first time, he thought, Sandra was wearing the lime-green Cozee Dayz tracksuit he'd given her for Christmas (the main present, no less). She had two reasons for this, neither of which related to his approval or pleasure, nor indicated in any way her own:

1. It didn't matter how wet, dirty or ruined the tracksuit got because she would not be wearing the revolting thing ever again.

2. It didn't matter whether anyone remembered the tracksuit (this might even be a bonus), if questioned after the event, because she would not be wearing the revolting thing ever again.

Below the hotel, they turned right and made their way along the beach. As they approached the hire facility, a noisy, high-spirited flotilla of amateur fishermen was setting off; to the Tiles' satisfaction, it appeared to be heading in the opposite direction to Rhos Cove. Sandra had a feeling of ECT (Everything Coming Together), of the system working harmoniously, and her fingers tingled with an electrical excitement. Derek stepped onto the jetty. 'Greetings, Man Who Rents Boats.'

He remembered this customer. 'You've only got one. Didn't order two.'

Mrs Tile laughed, to her husband's irritation, and added unnecessarily: 'One's enough, thank you.'

Suitably encouraged, the boatman ran with the joke. A long way. He handed Derek a pair of lifejackets. 'One each, not both for you.' He then pointed at their reserved vessel. 'There's only one engine, one propellor, one wheel, one choke, one throttle, one gear lever, one can of petrol and one kill cord.' He held out a red lanyard with a quick-release fitting for the console and a clip at the other end. 'Know what this is? Alright then. Whoever's driving, tie it round your wrist or knee, it's up to you. But tie it somewhere... we don't want any accidents.'

'We don't,' Sandra agreed.

'And those are oars.' He looked at Derek again. 'You can have two of them.'

It was five past the hour when Sandra cast off, a bright orange lifejacket tastefully complementing her lime-green outfit, and they motored slowly away from the landing stage. At exactly the same time, Lee left his caravan, holding a small box decorated with a paw print, and headed down the track by the side of the meadow. He passed a middle-aged couple coming in the opposite direction; they'd never seen each other before. Gail said hello.

Mr Tile may have been driving the boat, but his thoughts were still on the jetty. 'You found him very amusing, didn't you?'

There was silence next to him for a moment. 'I didn't notice anyone else. Only the handsome ship's captain who's taking me to sea. The one with the nice legs.'

He looked at his legs. He'd done a pretty good job keeping himself in shape, he thought, all things considered. He smiled with self-congratulation, feeling powerful and reckless. 'Let's see how fast this baby can go. Hold on tight.' He pushed the throttle right forward; there was a subtle increase in speed, and the bow rose marginally in the water.

As a key actor in the ROMCOM (Remote Omnidirectional Communication), Mrs Tile had a leading role to perform. Lee had given her a quick demonstration of the walkie-talkies (range up to eight kilometres), familiarised her with the lingo he'd learnt working on a film set as a rigger earlier that year (before an unfortunate altercation with an "accusing" member of the cast), set both radios to the same frequency and suggested she choose a character for her call name.

Deciding it was time to play her part, she removed the yellow and black handset from its travel case – part of a special offer multipack of waterproof, easy-seal freezer bags bought for precisely this kind of eventuality – and switched it on. She pushed in the talk button to transmit, waited a second, then spoke: 'Walkie check.'

Pleasingly, there was an immediate, clear response: 'Walkie check good.'

'Woolf for Batman.'

'Go for Batman!'

'What's your twenty? Over.'

'At the beach. What's yours? Over.'

'On the water. Over.'

'Ten-four. Talk when I've got the boat. Over.'

'Ten-four. Woolf signing off.'

It appeared to the radio operator that the plot was progressing every bit as smoothly as their pleasure craft skimming across the surface of Burricon Bay at that moment. Had she also possessed the power of omniscience, as Derek in his more paranoid moments suspected was the case, within the same eight-kilometre range, Sandra would have become aware of several events in the next few minutes with mixed emotions: Gail and Bruce making steady progress on their walk round to the rendezvous, reaching the place on the track where the Tiles had encountered the hare; Lee, a broad grin on his face, being shown the boatman's RHIB (Rigid-Hull Inflatable Boat) with its powerful outboard on the back; and, not so agreeably, a family arriving in Rhos Cove by sea, delighted to find they had the place to themselves, beaching the boat and disembarking, the three children whooping with excitement and rushing off to explore, the parents establishing a camp on the shore that had all the signs of becoming a semi-permanent structure, certainly one that would suit their needs for the entire afternoon.

It took the Tiles longer than expected – another twenty minutes – to get round the coast, with the sea choppier and the pull of the currents much stronger out in the open water than the early stages of the trip. Although the slow progress was frustrating, the outbound journey did confirm the shrewdness of Sandra's decision to try and position the point of impact beyond the shelter of the cove.

As they approached the Mew Stone, the radio came to life: 'Batman for Wolf.'

'Go for Woolf!'

'I've just left… doesn't stop that bloke. Fuck me, can he talk. On and on he went. What's you twenty? Over.'

'Not far away now. Will keep you posted. Over.'

'Ten-four. Speak then. Batman signing off.'

Derek pointed the boat between the rocky outcrop and the headland, steering towards the mouth of the small bay which initially seemed to be clear of other vessels. It was only when they got further round the end of the promontory, affording a direct line of sight to the beach for the first time, that the first major obstacle of the afternoon presented itself. Mrs Tile removed the binoculars from their cold-storage travel case and instructed her husband to slow down. She scanned the shingle strip intently, changing her position and adjusting the focus several times; the situation looked challenging, from any point of view.

It was critical to ascertain whether the family's activity around their camp indicated the end of the arrival or the arrival of the end; regrettably, the answer appeared to be the former. To make matters worse, a man and woman she recognised had just emerged from the trees and were making their way along the beach in search of their own place to stop. The clock was now ticking. Sandra turned to the driver: 'Time for plan B.' Derek accelerated towards the shore, as fast as the craft would allow anyway. She spoke into the walkie-talkie: 'Woolf for Batman.'

'Go for Batman!'

'We've got a bogey. Need to lock it up. Move to plan B. Crew to standby. Over.'

'Ten-four. Over.'

'Woolf signing off.'

Mr Tile removed his lifejacket and gilet, then jumped out of the boat they'd moored in the shallows. With the radio in his hand, he waded ashore and walked across the pebbles towards the family's beach bivouac; he could see two young children playing in the sea further along. A man, woman and little girl were lying on the ground together. 'Greetings.'

The man looked up. 'Afternoon.'

The girl was staring at the newcomer. 'What does his shirt say, Mummy?'

'Lifeguard.'

'He's quite old.'

Dad tried not to laugh. 'He's a senior lifeguard. A lifeguard senior.'

The lifeguard cleared his throat and pointed, his arm and voice steady. 'I need you to ask those two to come out of the water. Right now, please.'

The man looked unimpressed. 'What for? You don't get great whites in Wales, Chief Brody.'

'No. But you do get lion's mane jellyfish. And we've had reports of them today in this cove.'

'Are they dangerous?'

'A child got stung here this morning. On the face. He needed hospital treatment. The sting of a lion's mane is so severe it can cause anaphylactic shock.'

Mum looked panic-stricken. 'Jesus Christ! Get the kids out, Peter. *Now!*' The man dashed off. 'What are they doing here?'

'We think this bay has become a breeding site. It's ideal in many ways and it's the right time of year. The beach is being closed for swimming. Or even paddling. They can still sting washed up on the shore… you've got a boat. I suggest you go round the coast. We've had no sightings there.'

'Thank you. That sounds sensible.'

Leonard nodded, once, heroically, in his opinion. 'Just doing my job, mam. You keep that little lady safe now.'

The woman gave him a quizzical look. 'I will. Thanks again.' She saw Peter coming back with the children in tow. 'Come on, gang, let's get packed up. We're moving on.'

The oldest skimmed a pebble across the water in irritation. 'Why do we have to go, Dad? It's our last day. I didn't see any jellyfish.'

'That doesn't mean they're not in the water. Besides…' he slung his son over his shoulder, 'they don't sell ice cream here.'

The hero turned to go; it was time to update headquarters. He spoke into the walkie-talkie: 'I'm on my way. All bathers clear of danger.' He strode off, the area secure and his task complete.

The radio crackled. 'Who the fuck is this?'

'Lifeguard.'

'It can't be. Lifeguard's a woman, mate.'

'All civilians are safe and the water evacuated.'

'Congratulations, Wonder Woman. Now give me back to Wolf.'

There was a short silence. 'This is Lifeguard.'

'No, it's not. Let's try it again. The superhero Lifeguard is female. And you're not. That means, by a process called logic, you can't be Lifeguard. Bat*man* signing off.'

Along the shore, Gail was lying on her front, watching the scene unfold with interest. Bruce lay on his back sunbathing; his eyes were closed. For some reason, Derek had stopped. He was standing stone-still on the beach, staring at the handset. On the boat, Sandra smiled – she could see plan B was working out. Now it was just a question of waiting. And hoping nobody else decided to visit Rhos Cove in the next twenty, crucial, minutes.

The family didn't hang around – their camp was dismantled and the boat loaded in a quarter of that time; they set off with a departing wave. Gail watched them go, calculating that when they reached the mouth of the bay it would be safe to start. As soon as the moment arrived, she shook Bruce awake. Mrs Tile observed them from behind her sunglasses – a discussion was going on. They both sat up and Gail pointed towards the Mew Stone; there was a formal handshake. Bruce seemed to notice something in the dunes, and she turned behind to look. He pushed her over, sprinted into the sea laughing, then frontcrawled away. Gail followed, with a quick glance in Sandra's direction. The action sequence had begun.

The second swimmer was about fifty metres from the shore, the first another fifty in front; on Sandra's signal, Derek started the boat's engine and pulled up the anchor. She picked up the walkie-talkie.

'Woolf for Batman.'

'Go for Batman!'

'The Penguin is in the water. Over.'

'Ten-four. Over.'

'What's your twenty? Over.'

'By the rock. Over.'

'Ten-four. Wait for instruction. Over.'

'Ten-four. Over.'

'Woolf signing off.'

The boat circled slowly round the cove, describing an arc in the sea as it tracked the two figures. The distance between them was about right as Bruce approached the bay's entrance. Then he stopped, turned and started treading water. Mr Tile let the engine idle and looked at his wife. 'What's going on?'

She was watching through the binoculars. 'He's letting her catch up... there's another problem.' Sandra could see a speedboat approaching with four adults on board. It was moving fast directly towards the mouth of Rhos Cove. 'We've got company.' The intruder raced past the swimmers into the bay and headed straight for the shore. It slowed right down, the bow sinking in the water and the craft rocking on its own wake. Sandra could tell some kind of debate was taking place between the driver and his passengers as he steered parallel to the beach. 'One of them wants to stay. Two don't. They're arguing... the other one's getting involved now... it's getting heated.' A decision was made. She saw the driver throw his hands up in frustration. The boat surged forward, turned sharply and sped back out to sea, giving a wide berth to a man and woman next to each other in the water. 'They've gone... what's she doing?' Something odd was happening: the woman was waving.

'What's who doing?'

'Gail. I think she's trying to get our attention... she is.'

They both heard a man's voice shouting for help. 'Are we going over, my love?'

'I guess so. She must have a reason... I'd better let Lee know.'

As they got closer, Derek recognised Bruce's voice: 'Over here! We need help!'

He drove to a position nearby and eased the throttle back. 'Greetings! What seems to be the problem?'

'Cramp!' Gail called. 'I can't swim!'

Mrs Tile understood: 'Do you want a lift to shore?'

'Please! My leg's gone!'

'Fast as you can!' Bruce instructed.

Mr Tile manoeuvred alongside and put the gear lever in neutral. Between them – one pushing, two pulling – Gail was hauled aboard. 'Thank you.' She immediately braced the ball of her foot against the edge and gasped. 'That really hurts.'

At this point, Bruce seemed to remember Derek from the night before; he let go of the side and paddled away. 'Do you mind if I don't come?'

Gail shook her head. 'No. Finish your swim. I'll be fine.'

'OK. See you back there.' He set off towards the Mew Stone without another word.

Sandra handed their passenger a towel. 'Very convincing.'

'Not bad, was it?' She stretched out her legs and rotated

the ankles. 'I had no choice. He wanted to do the last bit together… I'm struggling with something though, is that a tracksuit you're wearing?'

'Let's not go there. Cramp was clever.'

'I knew Bruce wouldn't get in the boat when he saw your husband. Be far too awkward.'

'How ironic, Mr Callous is going to die of embarrassment.' She checked for other vessels in the vicinity, then reached under the seat for the radio. 'Woolf for Batman.'

'Go for Batman!'

'The Penguin's lonely. Time to say hello. Over.'

'Ten-four. Going to make contact. Over.'

'Woolf signing off.'

The RHIB tore round the rock in a tight curve, its keel cutting through the swell, the engine roaring flat out with one hundred horses stampeding… too late, the swimmer heard them coming. Lee screamed above the noise: '*Oi! Wanker! This is for JJ!*' Bruce's last cognitive process in this life, before the rigid hull rammed into his head, cracking open the skull and floating his brains on the water like a jellyfish, was incomprehension. The last word Gail would ever hear Lee speak (the Tiles were able to discern him faintly in the caravan that night), as their boat gently slid onto the pebbly beach, was a cry of triumph that echoed across the cove: '*Kapow!*'

The box of ashes was emptied over the side of the RHIB out at sea; it was a solemn moment. The Tiles returned their boat to the jetty within the allotted time; they were even a few minutes early. Gail raised the alarm just before 17:30; she had actually been asleep. Bruce's body was found three miles down the coast that evening after an intensive search; the severe head trauma was consistent with a collision.

Two years later, Lee would go on holiday with friends to Ibiza and initiate a restaurant altercation over a tortilla. The dispute became violent; a waiter was punched. Unable to forgive the culinary slur, the chef/owner of the tapas bar would falsely identify Lee as the assailant to his cousin, one of the attending officers at the scene. He was arrested and a small quantity of cannabis found in his possession. In a remarkable piece of good luck, but demonstrating a commendable dedication to tackling the island's drug problem, the police came across a stash of ecstasy tablets simply sitting in the wardrobe when they searched his hotel room. During the investigation, an important eyewitness (another cousin) would testify that Lee was a well-known dealer on the club scene. Coincidentally, the pills which were found happened to carry the distinctive bat logo linked by the media to a number of recent tourist deaths. The alarmist nature of the coverage had put huge pressure on the Ibizan authorities, whose concern for public health was obviously paramount. Lee would maintain throughout the decade he served in a mainland prison that the witness was lying, and he'd been framed.

THIRTEEN

The next morning, after a pleasant walk on the beach with Benson and a light, healthy breakfast of yoghurt and fruit (the anticipated Sunday roast for lunch precluded anything more), the Tiles, like everybody else in the area who had hired a boat, were questioned about their movements the previous afternoon. Sadly, like everybody else, they'd seen nothing suspicious and were unable to help the police with their enquiries. One man in another local hotel did tell them a story about an odd, older lifeguard in Rhos Cove but he wasn't taken seriously. 'I don't think the man's injuries came about from a collision with a jellyfish, sir.'

On their way back to the caravan, Sandra peeled off to have a chat with her friend Gwyn on reception. She returned half an hour later to find her husband performing his weekend exercises in the living room. 'There's something we need to discuss.'

He was lying on one side, stretching in the other direction. 'Fire away, my love. Quite capable of holding a conversation at the same time.'

'No, you're not. Stop doing that please.'

'I'm in a position to talk. It may be non-standard, but interlocution is viable.'

'Bruce and Gail checked into the hotel as Mr and Mrs Humphries.'

He started the opposing stretch. 'Hardly going to give her own name.'

'They arrived together, in one car. She left first thing this morning in the same car.'

He stopped to process this information. 'It must be her car then... something's not right. Unless he was serving a ban, why on earth would she pick Bruce up?'

'That's what I thought.'

He sat up. 'We need the registration number of that vehicle. The hotel must have it. We had to give ours to reception.'

Sandra took a slip of paper out of her pocket and waved it in front of him. 'I'm ahead of you, Mr Tile.'

'How did you get that, Mrs Tile?'

'I told Gwyn you worked for the DVLA and with the number plate we could find out if they were actually married.'

Derek's expression changed. 'You shouldn't have said that. It's not right. The Department for Transport is my employer. That needs rectifying before we proceed. I'd like you to explain your error to Gwyn.'

'Don't be so ridiculous. It doesn't matter.'

'It matters to me. She is now under the misapprehension I work for the DVLA. Which I don't.' He crossed his arms. 'I'm going to withdraw my cooperation unless you correct the mistake. We can either go to reception or you can phone Gwyn on speakerphone.'

She did as he asked. They both listened to the dial tone. After a few rings, the call was answered: 'Burricon Bay Hotel, Gwyn speaking. How can I help?'

'Hi Gwyn, sorry to bother you. This is Sandra Tile here…'

Gwyn sounded excited. 'Hello, Sandra, how are you getting on?'

'We're just about to start actually. My husband Derek wanted a quick word. I've put you on speaker…'

'Of course. Hello, Mr Tile.'

He stared at his wife. She pointed at her leg. 'Greetings, Gwyn, how's the leg?'

'That's kind. Much better thank you. I'm getting around more easily now.'

Sandra scratched her ear. 'And your hearing, how's that?'

There was a pause. 'There's not a problem with my hearing. Why do you ask, Mr Tile?'

'Call me Derek, please. Why do I ask…?' Sandra shrugged. 'I ask that because… there's a physiological connection between them… sometimes an injury to the leg can result in damage to the ear. And vice versa. The ears are nature's stabilisers. We can't walk without them.'

'I've not heard of that connection before, Derek.'

'Have you not? Interesting… but you've heard of the expressions "deaf as a post" and "peg leg"?'

'I have, yes.'

'A peg in Middle English referred to a small post. And through early prosthetics, it came to be synonymous with the leg.'

'I don't follow.'

'The inner ear has two main functions: hearing and balance. Any damage usually affects both. Which can result in deafness and the loss of mobility... because you have to stay in one place, like a post. Or else you'd fall over. As you would with only one leg. Hence the two expressions. And why I asked.'

There was a longer pause. 'I've got to go now, Mr Tile. Nice talking to you.' Gwyn put the phone down.

Derek went to fetch his work laptop and Sandra made some coffee, thereby both tacitly accepting this was to be an IND (Incident Not Discussed); they chose to focus on the car puzzle instead. He set up the computer on the kitchen table, logged into his DfT account and accessed the DVLA's vehicle registration database. 'Time to find out what's going on.' She sat down with two mugs and passed him the slip of paper. He entered the number plate into the system. The result came back:

GREY AUDI A6. REGISTERED
KEEPER: MR BRUCE HUMPHRIES
13 BEESTON FIELDS DRIVE,
NOTTINGHAM NG9 3DB

The driver's licence photograph showed it was the same man. Mrs Tile stared at the screen. 'I don't understand. How can it be his car?'

'If she drove it from the hotel, Gail must be a named driver. Which doesn't make any sense, I agree.'

'Maybe she's not. Can we check the insurance details?'

Mr Tile shook his head. 'Only whether the vehicle has valid insurance cover.' He went to a link. 'Which it does. Fully comprehensive cover.'

'So, we're none the wiser.'

'While we're looking…' He navigated to another part of the site. 'Bruce isn't, wasn't, banned either. No endorsements even.'

Sandra sighed. 'Nor an explanation.'

'There is something else we could try: cross-referencing the address to see if any other cars are registered there.'

'Can we do that?'

'We can, my love.' The search produced another number plate which Derek entered into the system. The result came back:

> WHITE MERCEDES GLA. REGISTERED
> KEEPER: MRS GAIL HUMPHRIES
> 13 BEESTON FIELDS DRIVE,
> NOTTINGHAM NG9 3DB

The driver's licence photograph showed it was the same woman.

*

A year later, Gail's solicitor would stand outside the inquest and give a short statement to reporters: 'Today the coroner reached a conclusion that Bruce Humphries was killed unlawfully. In legal terms, this ruling means his death was likely to have been due to a homicide offence. However, it does not seem likely that a person may be charged in relation to the offence.' She paused momentarily and glanced at the woman next to her. 'In emotional terms, today's ruling brings no respite for my client. Twelve months ago, Gail Humphries went on holiday as part of a happy, loving couple. She returned alone, without her husband… somebody knows what happened that afternoon. We urge anyone with information to come forward and contact the police. Thank you.'

Afterwards, the widow and her lawyer would walk to the car park together. Just the backs of their fingers touched.